CW00521619

WHY A REFUGE

Michael George

WHY A REFUGE

Stratton Press Publishing
831 N Tatnall Street Suite M #188,
Wilmington, DE 19801
www.stratton-press.com
1-888-323-7009

ISBN (Paperback): 978-1-64895-035-3
ISBN (Hardback): 978-1-64895-037-7
ISBN (Ebook): 978-1-64895-036-0

Printed in the United States of America

Also by Michael George

The Refuge series
Why A Refuge
Bridge To No Good
Grass Was Greener
To Save A Refuge

Finding Peri Gray
Of Rain Barrels And Bridges
Horses Lemons And Pretty Girls

For Marilynn
For all the years of putting up with me.
She has done a pretty good job of it.
For Bonnie and Tom
Life without them would be a whole lot less.

Contents

Prologue

The woman was in a hurry. She glanced out at the river through the window of the refuge office but gave it little of her attention, even though it shimmered golden brown in the brilliant afternoon sun. She made the call and, shivering with excitement, whispered, "I'm going to do it now. I can control him for five, maybe ten minutes, so hurry."

Her smile broadened, and still ignoring the river, she hung up the phone. If the river would speak, she could tell what really happened that day. Instead, the St. Catherine continued to do what she's always done, provide water for this land of refuge.

The St. Catherine River begins her journey to the refuge as a tiny stream, gurgling out of what was once a spring-fed marsh but is now a farm pond. It was dug years ago by a wise old farmer to provide a watering hole for his pastured cattle. Cornfields surround the pond on three sides. A few acres of small trees stand to the north but are cut so frequently for firewood that few of them ever mature.

The river lives in a land stranded between what was once the great woods, covering most of the eastern United States, and the open prairie, stretching west to the Rocky Mountains. It was once a land filled with endless marshes, oak savannah, and woods. A land teeming with life. A land changed, then forgotten, by the humans who destroyed most of what it was. Only the St. Catherine remembers what it had been so long ago.

Still, she continues to wind her way south through farm fields and wood lots. Occasionally, before she grows from a stream to a river, she is hidden in one of the remaining low ground swamps or ponds, although there are few wetlands remaining. Most were drained for farmland. Those surviving are polluted with farm chemicals, producing little more than deformed frogs. Seldom is one even large enough to provide a home for a pair of migrating ducks.

That part of Minnesota is not a place for large corporate farms. The soil is poor, predominantly sand and gravel, and heavily littered with rocks. The fields are small. The weathered buildings on the existing farms show their age and the low incomes the farms provide. Even so, the results are the same. It is rare to find a farm that doesn't use the same poisons and chemicals as their corporate brethren.

As the St. Catherine travels farther south, growing constantly, so do the size of the farms, the buildings, and the fields. But the flat and often low land, with patches of trees scattered here and there, changes little until the river passes through the town of Glentago. There she enters the refuge. In this place, the St. Catherine once again fulfills her original destiny. Dikes, water control structures, and refuge employees now control the depth of the water in lakes, ponds, and the marshes, but the river supplies the water. As she was in the past before man interfered, she is the mother of the wild land. Without her, there would be no Clayborne National Wildlife Refuge. No homes for the vast array of wild creatures. No sanctuary for the frequent human visitors.

On that hot August Saturday afternoon though, with the temperature in the mid-nineties and the humidity almost a hundred percent, the refuge was deserted by visiting humans. Only two refuge employees were there, hiding from the heat inside the air-conditioned offices of the refuge headquarters. They spent most of the morning arguing over some paperwork, then became friendlier as the day wore on.

Outside, there was little activity among the birds, squirrels, and other wild creatures. Even in and among the trees, the heat was oppressive. With no wind, the only sound was the buzz and hum of insects. If there had been visitors out in the quiet, it would have seemed to them to be a day when nothing could possibly happen.

They would have been wrong.

WHY A REFUGE

A car, moving fast along the gravel road, swerved into the headquarters' unpaved parking lot. It came to a sudden stop, raising a cloud of dust. With their tranquility disrupted, the wild creatures took up a noisy chatter. A large hulking man got out of the car and rushed inside the headquarters. The animals grew quiet as the dust settled. The near silence continued until a gun went off inside the building.

Outside, the gunshot made a sound like a muffled explosion coming from deep in the ground. Even so, it was loud enough to scare the birds out of the trees and start the squirrels chattering, chasing them high into the trees where the birds had been. The sound traveled only as far as the bend of the river flowing by.

There, the St. Catherine turned east, forming a large pool where she moved past the refuge headquarters. She narrowed again at an ancient steel bridge, turned southward, and continued her normal passage silently. The hulking man hurried out of the building and into his car, speeding away over the river bridge. He followed the road west, with dust billowing high over his car, leaving a dirty cloud hanging over the road behind it.

Life resumed its tranquil pace as birds returned to the trees. Squirrels softly chattered to each other while scampering among the trees and on the ground. A whitetail deer wandered by, stopping for a few moments to clean up the grain and seeds scattered off the backyard feeders by greedy birds searching for the most select morsels.

The serenity of the wild creatures was again shattered when a sheriff's car raced up the road from the east, its siren wailing and lights flashing. It turned into the parking lot. A young deputy got out of the car, rushed to the building, and went inside. Dale Magee stopped in the reception area.

"Where..." he started to ask the woman there, who appeared to be hysterical. Before he could finish his question, she answered with a frantic wave of her hands, pointing toward a hallway leading to the back of the building.

As Dale entered an office at the end of the hall, he swallowed hard, trying to control his stomach. Inside, a man was slumped in a chair behind a desk. It appeared that he had pushed the gun he was holding into his mouth, then pulled the trigger. It left the shelves behind him an ugly mess.

Dale quickly checked to be certain the man was dead. He tried to find a pulse, couldn't, then looked at his eyes. The pupils were fixed and dilated. The man was definitely dead. Because the young deputy was the first cop on the scene, he was nervous and not completely sure what procedures to follow before the sheriff arrived.

Violent suicide wasn't common in this part of rural Minnesota. This was the first time he'd been at the scene of one alone and the only time he'd ever been to one of a man so well liked and so prominent in the community. Suicide was always a shock. When it was a man of this caliber, it was incomprehensible.

Dale knew he shouldn't disturb anything and wanted to leave the room to wait for the sheriff. He didn't because he had a problem with returning to the reception area. He didn't want to deal with the hysterical woman waiting there. Confronting her, he was certain, would be more difficult than facing the horror in front of him. Dealing with women in any capacity wasn't something Dale Magee did well. Trying to cope with a beautiful woman who was so upset seemed, at the moment, to be an impossible task. So he took a notepad out of his pocket and looked around closely, moving around as little as possible. He noted the date, time of day, where he was, and where in the building he was. He made a quick sketch of the room, the locations of doors and windows, the desk with the body behind it, and everything else that had the slightest chance of being relevant.

Gradually, he began to think something was wrong with the room, that something seemed out of balance. He wondered if the death should be assumed to be a suicide or treated as a possible homicide. He did know they should do as much as possible to prove exactly what happened. The office was meticulously neat and organized, except for the records on the shelf behind the dead man. The mess the gun made when it blew away the back of the man's head wasn't what caught Dale's eye so much as the records themselves. They were dumped on the shelf with no apparent organization of any kind. Dale wanted, in the worst way, to examine those records but knew it was the one place in the office he shouldn't touch. Fingerprints could easily become important in a case like this. But he managed to get close enough to read the label on the folder lying on top of the pile, saying Impact Study.

He added that bit to his notebook, then continued his search for details. He soon noticed an empty spot on one of the bookshelves near the desk. Looking closer, he found a round spot there, surrounded by a bare hint of dust. A few feet away, he found a small shard of glass embedded in the carpeting. He picked up the glass, bagged and labeled it, and put it in his pocket. Next, he found a wet tissue in an empty wastebasket. He was about to pick it up and bag it when the sheriff stormed in.

"Jesus H. Christ," he said loudly, with no shock in his voice, "what a mess!"

"It is, Elmer," Dale agreed. "I thought I was going to lose it when I first got here. My stomach still hasn't settled."

"I can understand why. This is ugly." His mouth twisted into a minor grin. "Suicides like this are always messy. You haven't touched anything, have you?"

"No, but it doesn't seem to me that this is necessarily a suicide. Something about it doesn't feel right."

"What's to seem right about a suicide, Dale? It's always a dirty business. In all my years in this job, I've never seen one that wasn't."

"That's true. For some reason though, this one feels different. This office doesn't look quite right, and suicide isn't something I'd have thought Ray capable of. It's really out of character for him."

"Listen, Dale, it's like this. You wouldn't know a suicide from a wedding. You just ain't got the kind of experience you need. I been around a long time. A real long time, and what we got here is about as obvious a suicide as I ever seen in all my days of law enforcement. So save your feelings for the time they might be useful. This sure ain't the time. Right now, we got a lot of painful things to take care of. So go outside to put in the calls, we don't want that poor lady in the other room to have to listen to that, distraught as she is. Get the coroner and a couple of deputies out here. Then find Ray's home address so we can go over there later to tell his poor widow what went down.

I'll run this investigation and I'll ask the questions. I sure can't see you getting anything out of that terrified lady who found this mess."

"But..."

"No buts, Dale, just get to it."

Dale went out to make the necessary calls, even though he didn't approve of the way the sheriff was handling the investigation. He paused a moment by his car, taking a deep breath and filling his lungs with the fresh air of the wild land around him. He wondered why the sheriff refused to listen. He wondered, even more, why a man who spent his days in such a beautiful place would want to kill himself.

Dale loved his job, but he was certain that managing a wildlife refuge was as good a job as anyone could ever want. He knew Ray Foss well enough to know he loved his work and that he was also a happy family man. Even though Ray wasn't rich, Dale believed he had had it all. All any sane person would want, anyway. For those reasons, Dale had a difficult time believing Ray would kill himself.

He sighed, completed the calls, and went back inside. The sheriff was talking quietly to the woman who found the body. It took a moment before they noticed him. When they did, the sheriff didn't acknowledge Dale's presence, although his tone of voice changed.

Dale continued to listen, trying to commit everything he heard to memory so he could write it down later. He knew it was important for him to remember everything he could. How else would he ever figure out what really happened to such a good man on this hot August day?

Chapter 1

Mack Thomas was happy to be leaving the hospital, even though paying the bill took almost every cent he managed to save during five years of chasing rodeo. He walked to the downtown bus depot, bought a ticket for home, stashed his rig and suitcase in a station locker, then went out into the muggy, late afternoon air. He found a small cafe a few blocks later, with a sign in the window advertising chili on special for a dollar a bowl. He sat at a table near the back, as far from the other customers as he could get.

The waitress, who dropped a battered menu in front of him, forced a smile from her haggard face, which only made her look a lot older than she was. Mack returned the almost friendly smile, then ordered a bowl of their "on special" chili. She nodded an acknowledgment to his order, left, then returned in minutes with his food. She paused to watch him add a heavy layer of red pepper to the mass of beans, onions, and tomatoes. There was no evidence of meat in it.

"It's plenty hot the way it is," she said.

"I expect it is," he agreed. "Thing is, I've got a lot of hospital taste to get rid of."

"That right? You in very long?"

"Almost three weeks."

"Bull rider, huh?"

"How'd you know?"

"Rodeo left town about then. You got cowboy written all over you, and bull riders are usually the ones what get bad enough hurt to need a hospital stay.

"You must be a fan if you know all that."

"No way. My ex-old man rode. For about ten years before I got sense enough to give him the boot. Wouldn't of needed to the way things turned out. He got hisself killed less than a year later. Lucky for me, he never did get around to changing his insurance. Gave me something for all them wasted years I spent hoping he'd quit. Which bull did the damage?"

"Twiceback," Mack said, hoping she'd go away. He'd heard everything she had to say before.

"He's a mean one," she continued, and Mack knew the conversation with her wasn't going to end until he finished eating and left the place or another customer needed her services. So he ate as fast as the fire in the bowl would let him, only half-listening to her constant chatter. "It's a wonder they keep him around as many cowboys as he's hurt."

"Not really," Mack answered, after swallowing a mouthful of chili and gulping down some water. "The crowds love him." And, he thought, rodeo is no different than any other sport. Crowds are money, and money is more important than any of the players. There's always someone new wanting to play.

The truth was, though, he loved all of the rodeo animals. Especially the bulls. They were no different than he was. They simply did their jobs to the best of their ability. And no one in rodeo had more ability than the bulls. Certainly not Mack Thomas, the barely adequate bull rider.

"Still don't make no sense to me," the lady said, staring at his long silence. "When did he get you? His first time going after you or on his second try."

"His second."

The question brought back the memory of the ride that put him in the hospital. It was the third time he'd ridden the bull. He'd managed to stay on the full eight seconds the first time he'd ridden Twiceback. It was a small rodeo in Wyoming, when he and the bull were both new to rodeo. He was thrown the next time he drew him but landed clean, and the clowns kept him clear. This last ride, Mack was thrown immediately out of the chute and came down hard. He managed to dodge the bull in his first attempt to hit him. He wasn't so lucky when the bull charged him again. Not even the clowns could get between Mack and the bull fast enough. He could still feel the pain as the bull's head slammed into the small of his back. Twiceback. A perfect name for the bull, the way he always tried to come back after a thrown cowboy a second time.

The last ride on Twiceback was enough rodeo for Mack. This was the second time he'd been injured seriously enough to need a hospital visit. Bull riding was over for him now, and he was going home. A place he missed a lot more than he usually allowed himself to admit.

He was grateful when another customer called the waitress, letting him finish his chili in peace. His second cup of coffee, brought to him by a suddenly busy waitress as she hurried by, reinforced his thoughts of home and his father. That last day home was still vivid. It was a simple goodbye. His father, Ben, gave him a slap on the shoulder, stuffed a hundred-dollar bill into his shirt pocket, and gave him a quick handshake. Not much talking. Only, "there'll always be room for you here, Mack, if you don't get rich off rodeo."

And he surely hadn't. Eighty-six cents was his fortune after he paid for his meal. Eighty-six cents from dead broke. He lit his last cigarette on his walk back to the bus station. He was close to the station and passing an alley when he heard someone rush up behind him. He turned to see an object swinging down toward his skull.

He ducked and stepped to the side at the same time. As the object rushed by him, he swung hard with his right hand. It caught his attacker high on the side of the face. The object dropped to the ground, making a metallic clang when it hit the sidewalk. The person who had tried to hit him with it turned and ran. He shook his head with total disgust as he watched the lone figure disappear down the alley. The incident made him realize how happy he was to be going home, where muggings and murders didn't happen.

Chapter 2

The Kingsburg State Bank's large meeting room was dominated by a huge oval table, made from black walnut and polished to a high sheen. Corners of the room were filled with green plastic plants. Expensive wildlife prints framed in polished brass were hung on the beige vinyl-covered walls. The room was tastefully decorated, yet it still held a bored, lifeless look, much like the faces of the five people sitting in the heavily padded chairs around the table.

They were hoping the meeting would end soon. It was running long, and although everyone was anxious to leave, Rodney Twilabee, the CEO of Lands Magnificent, the bank's parent corporation, still had a few important questions he felt needed to be answered.

"I know it's been a long meeting," he said, "and you're all in a hurry to get out of here so you can clean off your desks and go home. However, I have a few questions on your land acquisition problems before we leave. Jason," he said to the bank's commercial loan officer, "you're heading up this part of the project, so what's the latest on Ben Thomas?"

"Well," Jason answered, after rolling his upper lip between his teeth and chewing on his long mustache, "we've purchased two of the last five properties, two more have gone into foreclosure, and we're getting very close on the Ben Thomas farm."

"How close? You know his land is critical. It's the one acquisition we must complete before construction can begin. Without it, there might not be a project. The stockholders are getting anxious and so are we. How close are you, Jason?"

"Not close enough, obviously. Ben Thomas has scheduled an auction. At best, we'll have title in a couple of weeks. At worst, a month. The old fool is going to sell the farm at his auction. He has the mistaken idea he'll get more for it that way. There will be a minimum bid required, but it'll be under our original offer. I think we can anticipate a savings of about fifty thousand on the purchase price."

"A lot of good that does, when you consider the cost overruns from the constant delays. How is it we can work a deal with the Feds faster than one old man?"

"He's stubborn. He doesn't want to sell. It's taken a lot to get him in the position where he has to. If we weren't holding the mortgage on his place, I doubt we'd have gotten this far. That and the fact he's had a major crop failure two years running."

"So it's luck then," said Harley Anderson, running his fingers through his thick gray hair. "I gave him his first loan, long before I became president of this bank, and he always got a crop off his lousy piece of ground. No matter what. Drought, storms, almost anything."

Jason turned to the CEO, winking. "I guess you're right, Harley. We got lucky."

Everyone except Harley smiled at Jason's comment. Instead, he asked, "What was that about, Jason?"

"What was what about?"

"The wink. You aren't responsible for those crop failures, are you? I'm as anxious as anyone to get the project underway. Not, however, to the extent of doing anything illegal."

"I don't know what you're talking about. If blinking my eyes bothers you, I apologize. I haven't done anything to be ashamed of, though, and I resent your implying I have."

"I'm only trying to understand what you're doing."

"Yeah...well..."

"Fine." Harley's frown made deep furrows in his brow. "Now I have a couple of questions."

"And they are?" Twilabee asked, his irritation with Harley obvious in his voice.

"What about the environmental impact study? What's its current status? I realize we'll go ahead with the project whether or not we have one. I am concerned, though, about the reaction of the press if one isn't completed. We need public support, not public concern."

"I can answer that," Jason quickly said. "It's no longer as serious a problem as it was initially. People are pretty much tired of hearing about environmental nonsense. I think the average person is intelligent enough to realize how ridiculous the concerns of the preservationists are. Republicans have got people thinking the right way now. They've pretty much illustrated how senseless it is to waste resources the way environmentalists are constantly wanting to do. The conservatives have consistently demonstrated it, be they in politics, business, religion, or the media, that we need to utilize all our resources in order to maintain a strong economy. In short, the environment and the idiots worried about it are the last thing we should be concerned with when we have real problems. Only economic issues are relevant. People can't put bread on the table, they aren't going to want to waste valuable land and water resources on some environmental crud. What they want is jobs."

"Sounds like we got lucky again," Harley said, "considering the problems we'd be having if Ray Foss were still alive. Where I didn't know him personally, I knew him well enough professionally to know he'd never consent to an environmental impact study that was at all positive about the project. If he was still at the refuge, he'd be fighting us in every way possible. Legal, through the press, and any other way he could."

"I don't believe," Jason answered, smiling, "I'd ever call a man killing himself lucky. However, his doing so did alleviate some potential problems, even if those problems are no longer serious."

"You all believe then," Harley said, "that environmental issues aren't a concern and probably won't be?"

"We do," Twilabee answered.

"Then I don't have any more questions."

"I think," Twilabee said, "this concludes the meeting. Harley, can I see you in your office for a minute?"

"Of course."

When they entered Harley's office, Twilabee got right to the point.

"It's time to retire, Harley."

"What? Why?"

"The project is too big to have anyone involved who isn't one hundred percent behind it. You've put in over thirty years at this bank, and you've done a great job. Now you've reached the age we all look forward to. I'll be looking for your official resignation tomorrow. Of course, your retirement package will be exceptionally generous."

"Just like that, I'm out."

"That's how it works, Harley, when you're not a hundred percent behind the bank's business."

CHAPTER 3

Mack Thomas took the seat behind the driver when he boarded the bus. His legs were tired and the pain in his back had increased during the short walk to the cafe. It was almost enough to make him forget the mugger in the alley.

He knew the pain was something he'd have to adjust to. His stay in the hospital wasn't long enough for him to heal completely, and no amount of time would rid him of all the pain. His most serious injury was in his back, and it was the one worrying him. The rest he could live with without much problem. The doctor told him the back injury was permanent, and he'd probably need to avoid heavy work in the future.

He realized, though, that his negative thoughts weren't doing him any good, so he tried to push them out of his head. When the driver got on the bus, he'd eliminated most of them. He was thinking of home and seeing his father Ben again.

The driver was a fuzzy leprechaun of a man who looked like he'd be more at home selling hotdogs at a ball game than pushing that big flexible diesel-powered bus around. Yet he made it look easy as he skillfully slipped through the heavy rush-hour traffic and onto the freeway, quickly reaching a steady seventy.

He took a battered pack of Marlboros from his shirt pocket, lit one for himself, then offered Mack one. When he took it, the driver gave him the pack.

"Keep 'em," he said, his tone of voice telling Mack there was no point in arguing.

"Thanks" was the only answer Mack could come up with.

They rode in silence until the driver mentioned he'd noticed Mack's bucking rig while stowing everyone's gear in the luggage compartment.

"How've you done this year," he asked, "been a good season?"

"Not one I'd brag about," Mack answered, then told him the story of his ride on Twiceback and why it was his last season riding bulls.

"Never will understand how anyone has the balls to ride those suckers, anyway," the driver said, laughing softly.

"It ain't balls so much as stubborn and stupid," Mack answered, enjoying the driver's compliment.

"Bet it got you a lot of pussy, though," the driver said, laughing again.

They rode out the night then, talking quietly about bull riding, bus driving, and, of course, women. Mack told him all his stories about women, real and imagined. All the stories except the one that mattered. The one about his wife.

It was shortly after dawn, with the sun still low on the horizon, when the driver made a special against-the-rules stop on the highway to let Mack off, only a few miles from his father's farm. He lit his last cigarette from the pack the bus driver gave him earlier as the bus pulled back on the highway. It was time to quit anyway, he knew, but savored every drag off the cigarette until it was gone.

He walked with his back to the rising sun. As sore as his legs and back were, he felt better as he got closer to home. That is, until he saw the auction notice hung on a post near the driveway entrance.

In a very short time, the notice said, the farm and all of its contents would be sold. It meant the farm would be gone, along with most of Mack's hopes and dreams. He wondered then if it was true that you can never go home again. He was lost inside himself as he walked down the driveway, so he didn't notice his surroundings until he was close to the house. As he did, the strange sight around him jolted him back to reality.

Even though the fields held small patches of lush green, they were mostly filled with dead and dying plants. It was a sight unlike any he'd ever seen on his father's farm. Not even the worst drought caused as much damage to the crops.

Mack had never before seen him fail to get a crop. Why would he now? Ben Thomas loved the land and had always pampered and nurtured it.

Tons of manure from neighboring dairy and pig farms were hauled in to rebuild the worn-out soil during the first few years he worked the land. Every year since, one-fourth of the land went into cover crops, which were plowed into the ground to replenish the humus. No chemicals, either fertilizers or pesticides, were ever used.

A makeshift, yet effective irrigation system supplied enough water when it was dry. Weeds were controlled by mulching as many crops as possible and by cultivating and hand-hoeing the rest.

Mack remembered the year the hail came on Memorial Day. All of the tomatoes and most of the peppers were planted already, and nearly half the vine crops were up. Everything was damaged, almost totally destroyed. He and his dad replanted the vine crops, then spent endless hours out in the fields hoeing around the broken stubs of tomato plants, taking time to hand-water each of them. Over half of them came back. The only crop close to a total loss was the peppers damaged by the hail. That land was replanted in summer squash and yielded heavily.

So what could be causing this crop loss? It made no sense. Most of the plants were dead or dying, while those still alive looked as healthy as ever. It did explain though, why there was an auction notice. Crop losses like this would break his dad financially.

Despite his concern, Mack couldn't help smiling when he walked around to the back of the house. Parked near the barn was an old green Chevy one-ton, with Texas plates. Its stake sides, topped with a white tarp, and its brightly polished green paint and chrome bumpers glimmered in the early morning sun.

Sitting on the ground, his hat pulled down over his eyes, with his back resting against one of the truck's old-fashioned, wide, white-wall tires, was his Uncle Roy.

"What brought you home, Mack?" he asked, without moving his hat or looking up.

"Bad ride on Twiceback," Mack told him, dropping his suitcase and bucking rig on the ground and sitting down on the suitcase. "Where's Dad?"

"Checking what's left of the tomatoes, I expect. He'll be wanting to pick what he can while he can. It ain't likely the son of a bitch who gets this place will do any more than plow them down."

"I guess I should go find him."

"You might as well wait here. He'll be back shortly. The bull bust you up pretty good?"

"It could've been worse. It's enough to end my rodeo days is all. Tell me, what brings you so far north?"

"I came to buy a saddle. You had breakfast?"

Mack shook his head no. Roy took a can of beer from the cooler next to him and tossed it to Mack. He took a couple of swallows, downing half of it. Roy grinned.

"You put it down some better than I remember. Rodeo does teach you how, doesn't it?"

"It does."

Roy leaned back again and was quiet. Mack knew it was like him to not talk much. Roy helped raise him when his mother died. That is, when Roy was there. It wasn't his way to stay around long. Only long enough to help Mack's dad, Ben, when he needed it, whether it was to get the crops planted, harvested, or anything else that needed to be done. It seemed as though Roy always showed up when Ben was in a bind, and this time was no exception.

A lot of people thought Roy was somewhat of a bum. Those who did didn't know him the way Mack did. Roy could work with any man, anytime, and always had whatever money he needed. He just never seemed to need much.

People also thought that Roy and Ben didn't get along. They constantly bickered about nearly everything. Politics, religion, horses, women, farming, even Fords and Chevrolets. They rarely agreed when someone else was around. Mack knew a different side. Most nights when Roy was there, the two of them stayed up late, talking quietly, drinking coffee if there was work the next day, whiskey if there wasn't. There was never a harsh word between them.

Roy gave Mack his first horse. A ratty old bucking bronc. He told Mack he could keep it if he could ride it. It took Mack a week to get a saddle on it, and another month went by before he rode it without being thrown as soon as he got on its back. When he finally rode it, Roy told him he could ride rodeo someday if he wanted to, even if he was built all wrong for it. His body was too long for his short legs, which made him too top heavy to be the best rider.

Mack put it off a few years. When he finally decided to go, Roy told him he might be too old to start, but there wouldn't be any harm in trying. Mack knew Roy was right. If he'd started younger, he might have won more than just enough prize money to pay his travel expenses, entry fees, and hospital bills, yet he knew from the beginning that he'd never be good enough to be a champion. Winning wasn't why he rode. He rode only for the thrill and satisfaction of the good ride when he made one. Someone else didn't need to lose for Mack to win.

Ben came in from the fields, his battered Ford pickup rattling loudly as he drove up next to Roy's Chevy.

"I take it," he said to Mack after he got out of the pickup and looked at his meager gear, "you didn't get rich off rodeo."

"Not quite," Mack answered, a broad grin filling his face, "but my neck ain't broke the way you said it'd be."

"Maybe not, but you sure ain't moving so good," he said as Mack pushed myself up to shake his hand.

"It could be worse."

Ben took Mack's hand and wrapped his other big callused hand around the back of Mack's neck, squeezing lightly. "Good to see you home, boy."

Mack smiled some more yet couldn't quite find the courage to give his dad the hug he knew he should. It was too far from the way they'd always treated each other. The handshake, neck squeeze, and smile seemed to be enough to tell them both how they felt.

"I saw the auction bill out front, Dad," Mack said as they let go and stepped apart. "What's going on?"

Ben gave Roy a quick look.

"No, Ben," Roy said, "I didn't tell him about it. Figured you'd want to."

"The auction's because I'm near broke. This is the second year running I've lost my crop. I don't know why. Doesn't seem to be any reason for it. One day, a field looks good, the next, it looks the way you see most of them now. I had county agent come out. He said he couldn't figure out what it was either."

"Isn't there some way you can hang on? I really hate to see you lose this place. Hell and damn, I hate to lose this place. I grew up here. Mom died here. It's home."

"No way that I can see, Mack. If I sell now, I'll about break even. If I hang on and I lose another crop, I'll be in way over my head. I'm getting too old to be walking around with nothing and with a load of debt on my head too. So it's best this way, to let it go now."

"Maybe we could hang on if I got a job and helped out. I owe you that much and more."

"You owe me nothing, Mack. Besides, I doubt the bank would ride with me on the part of the note due this fall. The way things are now, I think they want this place as bad as we want to keep it. Maybe even more."

"What for? This land's never been worth much."

"Why they want it, I don't know for sure. All I know is, they own most of the ground around here, and what they don't own, they will. Isn't but two or three farms left within a couple of miles either north or south. I'd guess most are gone from the other side of the refuge's south leg too."

"What the hell would they want with all the land?"

"Damned if I know."

"What if I talk to them? I might be able to help since Jason's still working for the bank. He's moved up the ladder some in the years I've been gone. We've been friends for a long time. I know he'll help if he can."

"You bet!" Roy said, getting up and walking away.

"Go ahead," Ben said, turning to follow Roy, "try it if you want to."

It was obvious to Mack that they didn't think much of his idea. But he was sure they simply didn't remember how close he and his friend Jason once were. They were still close enough, during the years he was gone, to exchange an occasional postcard. Mack had sent Jason one telling him that he was in the hospital and when he was coming home. So he decided to go see him right after he got a few hours of sleep.

A huge black cast-iron frying pan was already on the stove when he went inside the house. Bacon was sizzling in it, and Ben was pouring coffee into a mug for him. He picked it up after he sat down across from Roy at the large round oak table dominating the big kitchen. Even with Roy's face hidden behind his coffee mug, his frown was obvious.

Mack didn't mind him not saying anything. Roy rarely voiced his opinions without being asked. This time, Mack made the mistake of not asking.

Chapter 4

Mack didn't sleep long. The day was hot when he went to bed, and it was even hotter when he got up. He went directly into the shower to wash away the grime from his long bus ride, then dressed and took Ben's pickup to town. It was the same truck Ben owned when Mack left home, and it still handled the same. It's transmission linkage was sloppy, the front end vibrated, and it had a bad cough. It got him there anyway.

At the bank, he asked the pretty young receptionist if Jason Cheman was in and available. She smiled, as much at his Western-style clothes as out of friendliness. Then she put on her serious face and asked why he needed to see Jason.

"I want to talk to him."

"What about?"

"Tell him Mack Thomas wants to see him."

Her serious look turned to a frown. "I need to know your business, sir."

"It's as much pleasure," Mack said while reading the nametag she wore, "as business, Susan."

"I'm sorry," she said, sighing heavily to let him know he was wasting her time, "our loan officers are too busy to see anyone if it's not bank business."

"Look, lady…" he started to say, then noticed Jason coming out of one of the offices behind her. Rather than waste his time with the clerk, he walked over to Jason and held out his hand.

"It's been a while, Jason," he said.

"Yes, Mack," Jason answered, "it has been." The handshake felt fine, although Mack noticed Jason put a lot of effort into his smile and was doing his best to avoid eye contact. "When did you get home?" His voice carried some curiosity, but none of the feeling of friendship Mack expected.

"This morning. Like I told you in the card I sent, I got out of the hospital yesterday. I'm home for good. I thought I'd come by, say hello, and let you know I was back home. How's the family?"

"Fine. Mandy's working again."

"I didn't know she wasn't."

"She quit for a while after we lost the baby. She took it pretty hard."

"I didn't know about that either. Sorry to hear it."

"I thought you'd know." Jason looked surprised. "I thought Mandy wrote you about it."

"I haven't heard a thing from or about her since I started riding. You never wrote me about it. Dad isn't much for writing letters. The only contact between you and me since I left has been the few cards we've exchanged and the letter I wrote, telling you about my wife after she died."

"Well, I thought Mandy…" Jason stopped in midsentence.

Mack knew what he was going to say. He'd gone out with Mandy before she dropped him for Jason. He'd assumed Jason forgot about it a long time ago. It irritated Mack that he so obviously hadn't, so he let the silence hang between them until Jason spoke again.

"I suppose," Jason said finally, "you want to know the status of your dad's loan."

"I do."

"Let's go into my office."

Jason waited until they were seated before speaking.

"I want you to know, Mack, first and foremost, that I don't have anything to do with the way outstanding loans are handled. All I can do is what I'm told. The new owners of the bank look at the small commercial loans far differently than the way we used to. They don't like farm loans. They consider them unstable and unprofitable. They're not far from wrong, either, considering the number of farm loans we've had go bad. I know your dad's having problems with his crops, and although it's not surprising considering the low quality of the land he farms, I've still tried many times to get the bank to reconsider its policy in his case. They won't, and if I push it any further the only result will be my unemployment. Since I do need this job, my hands are tied. There's nothing I can do. Your dad will have to pay his note in full when it comes due this fall. There simply isn't any other way."

"This bank's always come out with Dad. So's anyone who's ever done business with him. Even when Mom was so sick for so long before she died, he paid the bills. It took him a lot of years, but he paid everyone. That's why he's still in debt. He's always paid anything and everything he ever owed. No matter what. And you know it! So what's wrong with this stinking bank?"

"Mack," Jason answered, his body stiffening and his face turning red, "This is neither the time nor the place for you to lose your temper. I'd have thought you'd have matured enough by now to know that."

"Maturity's got nothing to do with it."

"I'm not saying you're wrong about your dad or anything else. Nothing is going to convince the big city boys who own this bank. They didn't buy it to be nice. They bought it to make a profit, and it's their intention to maximize their profits. Your dad, and all farmers for that matter, no longer fit into their equation. For that, I'm truly sorry. I still can't do a thing about it."

"If it was the other way around, Jason, I'd do my best to find a way. And you know it."

"Mack, you have to understand. I really care about this job. I'm not going to throw it away on a lost cause."

"I can't see where it'd be any big deal if you did."

"Your attitude is no surprise to me, Mack. I'm married, though, and have my own responsibilities. I need this job. I can't run around chasing rainbows the way you do."

"No," Mack answered, hating the righteousness creeping into Jason's voice, "I don't suppose you can."

"No, I can't." Jason paused, a blank look covering his face as he gathered his thoughts. "I think you know that if it was up to me, your dad would have all the time he needs to cover his note. The problem is there honestly isn't anything I can do. All I can tell you and your dad to do now is to put your trust in the Lord. Faith can pull you through this. When you have enough faith, things always work out for the best."

"You bet."

"I can't believe, Mack, that you're still angry with God. Your mother died a long time ago."

"It wasn't only that she died. It was the way she was tortured before she died that I remember. So back off on the subject. Talking about it won't do either one of us any good."

"You sure haven't changed any, have you, Mack?"

"Yeah, I have. I'm older and a lot more beat up."

"Older maybe, but it doesn't seem to me that you've matured any."

"I guess it depends on how you look at it. I'm a lot wiser than I was when I started to rodeo. I just don't have any patience with bull-shit, and I'm not about to waste my time chasing beliefs or dreams that don't make any sense to me."

"Well, if you ever lost someone the way Mandy and I did when we lost the baby, you might understand better how much help and comfort faith can give you."

"You've known me long enough to know better than to say something so stupid. I was only ten when my mother died, and it wasn't much more than a year ago that my wife was killed. Your god didn't give me one bit of comfort when I lost either one of them."

"He would have, if you'd have asked for it."

"If he wanted me comforted, he wouldn't have killed them. Comfort would be having them around."

"That's pretty rash, blaming God for killing them."

"Why? You Christians claim God controls everything. If that's true, he's responsible. Otherwise, he sure isn't controlling anything."

"Look, Mack, even though I know you're wrong, I can't sit here and argue with you about it. I have other customers waiting and a lot of work to do. I'll talk to Mandy and find out what night we're free, then give you a call. You can come over for supper." Jason stood and stuck out his hand. "It's good to have you home."

"I wish I could say it was good to be home," Mack answered, taking Jason's hand and shaking it again.

Jason followed him out of the office and stopped at the desk of the young receptionist Mack encountered on his way in.

"Coffee time," Jason said to her.

Mack wondered if Jason thought he was out of his hearing, didn't care, or if he did it on purpose, trying to show Mack he still had a way with the ladies.

If he was trying to show Mack something, it didn't impress him and it was no big surprise. He'd known Jason long enough to know that no matter what Jason said, his primary interests in life were making it with the ladies and money. But not always in that order.

Chapter 5

Jason led the way to the small cafeteria in the basement, with Susan following about two steps behind him. They both poured coffee, each paying for their own. He went to a table in the farthest corner from the cash register. She pretended to hesitate a moment, then followed him to the table.

"Mind if I join you?" she asked, grinning. "We seem to be the only ones in here."

"Not at all, Susan," he answered. "I think I'd like some company right now."

"So," she asked, her voice muted, "was the jerk in the cowboy clothes related to Ben Thomas?"

"His son. I went to school with him."

"What did he want? He was in your office long enough."

"He wanted to know why I couldn't save his daddy's farm. If the fools knew how to handle their money, they wouldn't be losing their homes."

"You're right there. We made him a good offer on his farm. He should've taken it."

"Everything considered, it actually was a very generous offer. The fool wouldn't sell. Claiming he was doing exactly what he wanted to do and planned to keep on doing it. Now he's going to lose his precious farm. People like Ben Thomas should learn that doing what they want to do isn't nearly as important as taking care of their business is."

"With his attitude, he deserves his problems."

"His problems and more. He's got a lot of gall, giving me all this grief after we made him such a generous offer. It was nearly the full market value of his farm. When a man has his attitude, it's no surprise when he loses his crops two years in a row."

"You certainly have to wonder why he was so stubborn. I've seen his financials, and he never made much of a profit on his stupid farm. I heard somewhere that he never uses any pesticides or even fertilizer. There's no way anyone can farm that way."

"He's another ignorant environmentalist. Organic farming, he calls it. Total nonsense. It doesn't matter now, though, does it, Susan?" Jason said, trying to suppress a grin. "We're going to own his farm, and the project will continue."

"I just find it curious that he could be so stubborn, refusing to sell his farm for a project as important as ours." She paused to give him her best smile. "Are we on for tonight?"

"You bet. I'll call you when I get out of the house."

"Where are we going?"

"Same place as always."

"I sure wish, just once, we could stop somewhere in town here. I hate driving so far and then only having a couple of hours to spend with you. I hate all this hiding too."

"The time will come when we'll be able to do all the things you want to do."

"You keep saying we will, but you never tell me when."

"Susan, don't start with me. When...will be when I say it is. I have an important position to maintain here, so you should understand how careful I've got to be."

"I know, only I miss seeing my friends, and..."

"And what?"

"And I wish we could do more than go to the motel. Like out to eat or dancing. Even to the movies."

"You seem to enjoy yourself when we're together."

"You know I enjoy it. Yet..."

"Look, Susan, I know it's hard for you sometimes. Maybe Saturday night, if I can get loose early enough, we'll drive to the cities and do something. Okay?"

"Really try this time, please?"

"You bet. Now I've got to get back to work. I'll see you tonight."

Jason abruptly left the table, quickly walking out of the cafeteria. The conversation with Susan disturbed him. He knew it was time to dump her. She wasn't so great in bed anyway. It would be difficult for him to do now, though, because he'd be left with only two other women. Even three of them weren't able to give him the satisfaction he needed and knew he was entitled to. His wife Mandy was too rigid. His third woman, Elaine, allowed everything he wanted to do but was often too busy, either handling business for him or for the Washington people who planted her in the refuge to ensure that the project went forward. So he decided to wait and get rid of Susan later, after Elaine had more free time or Mandy learned to be a lot more submissive.

Assertiveness was definitely not a quality Jason appreciated in his women.

Chapter 6

The heat was brutal when Mack got back to the farm. It was in the high nineties, with Minnesota's normally high humidity. Ben and Roy were coping with it in their usual way. Roy handed Mack a beer from a large cooler on the ground after he sat down with them in the shade of a big oak tree in the front yard.

"It's entirely too hot," Roy complained.

"It must feel like home," Mack answered.

"It's never this hot in Texas."

"It usually gets hotter."

"It isn't the same, Mack. Air's different."

"Dryer there?"

"It's more than that. In Texas, this kind of weather feels right. Here it doesn't. Places ought to be what they're supposed to be. Minnesota's supposed to be nice in August. Now it isn't and it irritates me. What did you find out at the bank?"

"Jason says there's nothing he can do. The city boys who own the bank now don't like farm loans. I think he'd help if he could."

"I guess what you think is up to you."

"You don't believe he would?"

"Hell no!"

"Why not? He's always been the kind of man who tried to do the right thing."

"Mack, what he's been doing is trying to prove he's doing the right thing. When a man's forever doing that, you got to wonder what he's up to."

"You think Jason's up to something?"

"Him or someone at his bank."

"What could the bank be trying to do?"

"Exactly what, I don't know yet. Ben doesn't either. But we'd sure like to find out."

"That is for sure the truth," Ben said.

"Well," Mack said, "I'll be seeing Jason some night this week. He said he's going to call and have me over for supper. Maybe I can learn something then."

"That sounds like a fine idea, Mack," Roy told him, "but there's something I got to say since you apparently haven't learned it yet. It makes a hell of a lot more sense to have a good enemy than a bad friend."

"You think Jason's a bad friend?"

"He isn't a good one."

Ben took three more beers out of the cooler and passed them around.

"Too hot," he said.

It grew quiet, and the men let it take hold. Mack thought about what Roy said and the few words from Ben. Neither his uncle nor his father were suspicious men, preferring to take anyone they met at face value, never passing judgment without good reason. So Mack decided he'd find out what Jason and the bank were up to. Only the cackling of a few hens and the rustle of oak leaves filled the quiet until the third round of beer. Then Ben broke it.

"You got any plans, Mack?" he asked.

"None long term. For now, I'm going to hang around here to help you get ready for the auction. After that, I don't know."

"Maybe you ought to find a job. Roy and I will get done what needs to be done."

"I'm not quite ready for a job yet."

"What the hell are you going to do for money?"

"Worry about it later, after the auction. I've been broke before. I'll get by."

"I'll tell you what," Roy said. "I know how much your bucking rig would sell for here and what it's worth in Texas. I'll give you what it's worth here."

"You just bought yourself a bucking rig," Mack agreed, relieved to get some cash and believing it would be a long time before he saw Texas again. If Roy made a few dollars on the deal, it was okay with him.

Mack barely finished his last beer before the lack of sleep caught up with him. He stretched out on the grass and closed his eyes. Ben and Roy were gone when he woke up, and the western sky was filled with clouds of bright red and orange. He felt better than he had since his hospital stay. And the taste of it was almost gone.

Ben and Roy returned to the house as he was finishing another shower. Ben's pickup was loaded with vegetables, most of them tomatoes and potatoes. When he went out to help unload, they brushed him off.

"You look too pretty," Roy said, "all showered and shaved the way you are, to be working up a sweat."

"I don't have anything else to do," Mack countered, knowing the brush-off was more out of concern for his sore back than anything else.

"The hell," Roy told him, "the keys are in my truck. Haul yourself into town and find a willing female. You got the look of a man needing one. One thing, watch you don't go pushing down too hard on the accelerator. There's a lot more under the hood than you might expect."

Mack considered arguing, but the grins the two men carried told him he'd be better off keeping his mouth shut and leaving. And they were right. Since the accident that killed his wife Julie, there hadn't been anyone. More than a year was a long time.

So he left in Roy's truck. There was a day and night difference between driving it and Ben's old Ford. Everything was as tight as it was when it was new, and the engine was so quiet Mack had to concentrate to hear it. Only once did he press hard on the gas pedal. The truck snapped his head back against the rear window so violently, it scared him. The thing he liked best about the truck was the front seat. It later proved to be wide enough to accommodate him and a cute young lady when they spent some time stretched out on it.

Chapter 7

Jason was angry when he left the bank. He'd had a very bad day. First, he'd seen Mack Thomas, the last person Jason ever wanted to see again. Then something even worse happened. Harley Anderson was retired, and Gary Brown was made the new bank president. Jason should have gotten the promotion, and everyone knew it. He was the senior man, not Gary.

Jason was the one who handled the private land acquisitions while Lands Magnificent Corporation, the Kingsburg State Bank's parent corporation, was dealing with the Feds. Did it without arousing suspicion too. No one was ever able to figure out how he managed to force Ben Thomas to quit farming. Sure, the deal wasn't complete, but it was too close to matter now. There was no way it made any sense to him that he wasn't the one promoted.

His anger continued eating at him as he drove through Kingsburg, then south on the four-lane. Nine miles later, he turned right, drove west four miles, then south along a gravel county road. All the land on his left was fenced with four strands of barbed wire, with signs about every quarter mile saying Clayborne National Wildlife Refuge and that entering it was prohibited. Two miles down the dirt road, he turned left on a narrow road of loose sand, which ended at a gate for a refuge maintenance road.

Jason got out, pushed the unlocked gate open, then stopped to close it after driving through. Trees crowded the narrow drive until he came to a small clearing less than a mile later. A van belonging to the refuge was parked there. He got out of his car and climbed into the van.

"What gives, Elaine?" he asked the woman inside. "You're still dressed. I'm kind of short on time tonight. And what's with all that makeup? You know I don't like so much makeup."

"I'm even shorter on time," she answered, "and I'm wearing the makeup because I've got to go out with my darling husband tonight. I also have to see the idiot before I go home. You know I don't dare say no to him until this is over."

"Damn it, I was counting on it. I really had a bad day. I need to get relaxed."

"You know I can fix that. Open up. I'll relax you."

He unzipped his pants, and she took him in her mouth. A few minutes later, he was on the road, slightly more relaxed, and heading back to Kingsburg and home. His wife was in the kitchen preparing supper when he got there.

"Why isn't supper ready, Mandy?" he asked, feeling edgy again. "I have to work tonight!"

He was already anxious to meet Susan and get her in bed. Elaine hadn't totally satisfied him this time.

"I'm making pork chops," Mandy explained calmly, not noticing how edgy he was. "You always want them well-done and that takes time. I got home when I always do, so you know I haven't been home very long."

"You know, damn it, I don't like it when you give me sarcastic answers!"

"I wasn't being sarcastic. You asked why supper wasn't ready and I told you."

"I don't like you arguing with me, either." He slapped her hard across the face. "You should learn your place." He slapped her again.

She didn't answer and instead turned back to the stove, turning up the heat on the frying pan to ensure that the pork chops would be burned when she served them.

Chapter 8

Mack got home as the sun pushed its first rays over the horizon. While he watched it erase the stars, he realized he felt good enough to put in a full day's work.

After eating a big breakfast and taking a short nap, he went outside to start making repairs on the outbuildings. He knew he wouldn't be much good in the fields. Picking vegetables required too much bending and lifting for his sore back to handle. He could manage the minor repairs and painting okay, as long as he was careful about the way he moved. He was certain that any work done to the buildings would help bring a better price for the farm when it was auctioned.

The house didn't need any work. Unlike most men who live alone, Ben kept it in perfect order. Everything was scrubbed, vacuumed, and generally picked up, with plenty of fresh paint whenever it was needed. He never went to bed until every dirty dish was washed, wiped, and put away.

The work kept Mack busy enough to rid himself of his thoughts of Jason and the bank until a strange car drove in. He'd finished painting the old chicken coop and was down on his knees cleaning paint brushes, so he ignored the car, believing whoever it was wanted Ben.

She was standing close and looking down at him before he realized whom it was. He couldn't see much change in Mandy. She smiled as he looked up, and long ago yet still familiar feelings washed over him. As much as he'd tried in the years since they'd split up, he'd never managed to forget her. Her hold on him was still strong. He had never felt quite the same with any other woman. He didn't think he ever would.

He'd lost her, he believed, only because he couldn't be tamed and harnessed the way Jason was. It made him wonder, as it always did when he thought of her, whether or not he made the right choices. Then he realized she was laughing.

"Are you going to sit there all day with your mouth open," she asked, "or are you going to say hello?"

"Hi," Mack answered, suddenly wishing he could put his arms around her and hold her close. But it was something he didn't feel free to do, and even if he did, his clothes were speckled with wet paint. He settled for a light kiss on her cheek.

She pulled away sharply, her hand touching her cheek where he kissed her, drawing his attention to the large welt she was trying to hide with her makeup.

"Where," Mack asked when, for a fleeting second, he remembered his fist slamming into the side of a mugger's face, "did you get that, Mandy?"

"Oh, you know me," she said, making it sound like it was nothing, "clumsy as always. I banged into the edge of an open cabinet door the other night while I was doing the dishes."

If he had been thinking clearly, he'd have noticed that the edge of a cabinet door wouldn't leave a mark the same shape. But the thinking part of his brain was dead, overwhelmed by his feelings.

"So," he said, trying to say something that didn't sound too stupid, "did you stop to invite me to supper?"

"No," she answered, her look telling him he'd sounded as stupid as possible. "I only stopped to say hello. I think Jason would be quite unhappy if he knew I was here, not to mention if I invited you over."

Mack was embarrassed for having brought it up and tried to cover it by changing the subject. "Well, how are you? It's been a long time. You look great by the way."

"Thanks. I'm fine. Did Jason say something about you coming over for supper?"

"He mentioned it yesterday when I stopped in at the bank. Said he was going to check with you on what night."

"He didn't. The only reason he talked about you at all was because I asked him if he knew you were home. A friend of mine said she saw you in town or I wouldn't know."

"He probably forgot about it, given the busy schedule you two have."

"Not us, him. He's the one gone all the time."

"Really?"

"Yes, really. He says he's working. I know he's busy with the big project the bank's involved in, but sometimes I wonder. What can he be working on so late at night and on weekends?"

"I don't know. I've never worked in a bank. What kind of project is it?"

"I don't know much of anything about it. I think it might be some kind of resort. It's going to be tied into the wildlife refuge some way."

"How could it? They aren't supposed to use the refuge for anything except wildlife conservation. There's barely any hiking trails. Hunting season is about the only time people get to use it, and even then, most of it's still closed to the public."

"I don't know any of that, Mack. I quit paying attention to what Jason does a long time ago."

Mack wanted to know more, but before he could ask her another question, Ben and Roy came in from the fields.

"I better go," Mandy said as soon as she saw them, "I'm late already."

"You've only been here a couple of minutes, Mandy," he said, wanting her to stay at least long enough to answer his questions.

"Jason doesn't like it when I'm late."

"Okay, I understand. Can I see you again?"

"I don't know. Maybe." She left suddenly, and he watched her drive away before going over to help Ben and Roy unload the truck.

"Was that Mandy?" Ben asked.

"Yes."

"What did she have to say?"

"Not a lot. She mostly stopped to say hello. But she said one thing I found curious. Jason's working on some big project for the bank. She said it's connected with the refuge."

"I wouldn't put too much stock in it. I've heard those rumors too. It's about all they are I think. It isn't likely anyone's going to mess with the refuge. It means too much to people. So how was Mandy? How'd she seem?"

"Okay."

"Just okay? Well...that's good."

Roy stood quietly while Ben and Mack talked. He hesitated when Ben went back to unloading, looking as though he wanted to say something. Mack caught his eye for an instant and saw a sad knowing look. Roy kept quiet though, and went back to work. Mack followed, and it was quickly, if silently, done. Mack stayed outside until it was time to eat.

Supper was simple. Burnt hamburgers and canned corn, fried in the hamburger grease. It, too, was eaten in virtual silence. Ben was a good cook, and it was unusual for him to just slap together a meal. And it was almost unheard of for Ben and Roy to eat in silence. Meals were always talking time for them.

As soon as they finished eating, Ben brought out a bottle. A good Kentucky bourbon. He held it up for Mack, who shook his head no. Ben shrugged and poured for Roy and himself. Water glasses half full. Roy took a healthy swallow, then picked up a dishcloth and started wiping dishes as Ben washed. It surprised Mack to see him do it. He grew up watching Roy do every kind of work there was around the farm but never the dishes. It was too much for Mack.

"You two want to tell me what's wrong?"

"Nothing to tell," Roy answered softly. Too softly.

"You know I'm not going to buy that, Roy."

"There's nothing to buy."

"I wish one of you would tell me what's going on."

"Why do you think something's going on?"

"Because of the way you're acting. First, you hurry supper, second, you don't talk, third, I've never seen either one of you drink hard stuff when you've got work to do in the morning. And this is the first time in my life, Roy, I've ever seen you do dishes."

"There isn't any work to do tomorrow, Mack," Ben answered, speaking slowly. "Least ways, none that's got a rush on it. Everything's in from the fields. The rest of the crops are gone."

"I knew it was bad, but I didn't think it was that bad. There's something else wrong, though. What is it?"

Roy heaved a big sigh. "Look, Mack, you know I'm not much for telling anyone what to do. Your dad, either. We think, though, that maybe you ought not be seeing Mandy."

"I'm not seeing her, so if that's what's bothering you, you can forget it. The only reason she stopped by was to say hello. I didn't know she was coming."

"Okay, Mack," Roy said, turning back to the sink.

Mack wanted to continue the conversation and would have, but it was obvious Roy didn't. He had too much respect for Roy to push it. To ease his frustration, he went outside. He walked around the yard, through the outbuildings, then across the fields toward the refuge, getting there before he realized it.

He walked south along the refuge fence line awhile, noticing as he did that the fence wasn't maintained very well. The bottom strand of barbed wire was down and the next one up was coming loose in spots. Other than the fence, things looked as they always had.

When he came to an old wildlife trail, one he had walked many times as a kid, he climbed the fence and followed it. It took him through a large stand of pines planted by farmers during the depression years, before the federal government bought up the land to create the refuge. He immersed himself in its cool, clean air and fresh pine scents, wishing life could be as simple and clean as this spot was. The trail wound up a long hill, serving as a high bank for the St. Catherine River. The climb made him sweat heavily, and he was tempted to undress and take a swim when he reached the river. He satisfied the urge by splashing his face with its shallow, somewhat muddy water, then followed its lower bank back north. As he walked, he wondered about the project Mandy mentioned. He was sure it had to be some kind of resort. How could it possibly use the river valley?

The river itself was too shallow for boating or swimming. The fishing was lousy, except for a short time in the spring when the Northern Pike made their spawning run. The terrain was too rough for snowmobiles, and the hills weren't high enough for skiing. About all it offered was bird watching and nature walks. How could a resort stay in business with only those activities to offer? It made no sense, so he pushed it out of his mind and concentrated on his surroundings.

It wasn't long before his attention was rewarded. A red fox burst from a clump of bushes a few feet in front of him. Next, he surprised three whitetail deer, two does, and a fawn, feeding in a clearing a short way up the riverbank.

He slowed his walk even more and began to see squirrels playing high up in the oaks, then a huge bull snake skittered across the path. Birds were everywhere. He even caught a glimpse of a scarlet tanager, his springtime bright black and red colors faded this late in the summer.

He followed the river until he reached the end of its high banks, near the county road. The land there flattened out, and the main part of the refuge, on the other side of the road, spread east and west as it ran several miles north. He stopped to rest a moment, taking in as much of the refuge as he could, remembering the times he spent there as a kid. He and Jason. At one time or another, they explored every acre of the refuge. All thirty thousand of them.

Technically, they weren't supposed to go in there the way they did. Only the refuge staff was allowed to, except in specific designated areas. Over time, the two of them got to know everyone who worked there. Since they were careful not to damage or harm anything, they were quietly ignored. All of the refuge seemed to be their own private world then, but they both loved the narrow south leg bordering Ben's farm the most. Its rugged terrain discouraged other trespassers, leaving it to them almost exclusively. Even the refuge staff stayed away most of the time because the land was too rough for any of the wetland pools that needed to be monitored and controlled. It also was considered less important than the rest of the refuge since it didn't support much waterfowl.

It was a good place to grow up, a good place to be a kid, and for a fleeting moment, Mack wished for those days again. But they were gone and the sun was low on the horizon, so he turned toward home.

Roy and Ben were in the living room, talking softly when he went inside the house. The bottle, half gone now, was on the coffee table between them. Mack stood quietly in the dark, watching them for a moment. Ben was sitting in his heavy, overstuffed easy chair, in the far corner of the room, close to his books. They filled several sections of floor to ceiling shelves along both walls behind him.

"They're like good friends, most of them," Ben had said more times than Mack could remember.

They were good friends to Mack too, and he'd gotten most of his education from them, from his hours exploring and working in the refuge, and from Ben and Roy. After the sixth grade, school was little more than a place he was forced to go. When he started collecting his books on wildlife, ecology, and the environment, Ben and Roy built another shelf unit in the room, so he'd have enough room to store them properly. After it was installed and filled with his books, Roy told him quietly, "I'm real glad you're reading so much, Mack. I never got shit out of high school, either. I never figured it to be much more'n a human holding tank."

Roy was gently rocking in the heavy oak chair he'd built for Mack's mother, only days before Mack was born. Roy built it, he told her, "So you'll have something, Sarah, to rock the boy to sleep in." Roy was the only one at the time who knew Mack would be a boy.

Mack sighed heavily, and they looked up in his direction. He gave them a wave, then went up the stairs and to bed. They kept their voices low, so muted, Mack couldn't pick up a trace of their conversation. He hated the quiet now. It intensified the growing knot of an undefined fear creeping into his belly.

Chapter 9

"I'm really worried about the boy," Ben said softly, as soon as Mack was upstairs.

"He'll heal, Ben. Mack's grown up to be a strong man."

"I wasn't referring to his injuries. There's something troubling him. Something deep down that he's not talking about."

"I know. I've seen it in his eyes. He tries to hide it, but it's there. He's been having some bad dreams too. I hear him at night when I get up to make my every night pee call."

"I sure do wish he'd talk about it. He'd heal faster if he did."

"That's a lot to ask, Ben, considering the way we raised him. Neither one of us has ever been much for talking about what's inside."

"We talk to each other. Almost always have, except…"

"That time doesn't count, and we got over it. We're brothers too, Ben. Mack doesn't have a brother. He doesn't have much for friends either."

"That's true. He never had anyone, except Jason, that he called a close friend. We both know what a devious son of a bitch he's always been."

"We taught him to be careful about laying judgments on people. Maybe with Jason, he was too careful."

"You're right about that, Roy. There's more, though."

"He'll talk about it in time. It wouldn't be like him, being home such a short time after being gone so long, to talk about his problems. Especially not now when he's so worried about you. It's not like Mack to be concerned about himself first. If it was, he'd of started riding rodeo right out of high school instead of waiting so long to go. He only stayed home, you know, for you."

"I thought it was Mandy who kept him here."

"Sure, it was her. Mostly, I think, it was you he was thinking of. His going at all is likely part of what's bothering him now, given the situation you're in."

"Now I feel worse than ever, Roy. I don't want him worrying about me. All I want, all I'll ever want, is for him to have a good life, no matter what it is he does. Most of my life I've done what I wanted and had what I wanted. About the only really hard thing I've ever dealt with was losing Sarah."

"That isn't going to change his worry any, Ben. Mack's got too big a heart to be worrying about himself right now."

"What can we do for him? Seems to me, we ought to be doing something."

"We're already doing for him, what he mostly wants us to do."

"What…exactly is that?"

"We're here for him, Ben. We're all the family he's got, and we're here. It isn't everything, it's just the best we can do right now."

"Yeah, it's a start, and like you said, no matter what, he's a strong man."

"You've got that right, Ben."

Chapter 10

Slowly, ever so slowly, the coffin was lowered. Only a few were there for the service. Her parents, her sister, five cowboys, and Mack. The others were gone now. Off somewhere for coffee and cake. A place for the parents and sister to cry and for the cowboys to get real uncomfortable. Only Mack stood watch. He and the sad-faced man in the red flannel shirt who was turning the crank to lower her into the hole in the dry desert ground. The man tried to wait until Mack was gone so he wouldn't be there to watch. He couldn't wait any longer. It didn't matter. Mack told him it didn't. He needed to watch until the first shovel of dirt was thrown in the hole.

"Julie!" Mack screamed. "Julie...no!"

His own voice yanked Mack out of his dream. He bolted upright in bed, snapping something in his back. A sharp pain seared through it. He groaned as he opened his eyes. Everything was blurred, so he wiped the back of his hand hard across them. Pain again screamed through his back. He slowly lay back down to relax the tightly bound muscles.

Ben knocked on the bedroom door, asking, "You okay, Mack?"

"Yeah," Mack answered, struggling to keep his voice even, "I'm fine."

Ben hesitated and then walked away. Mack stayed where he was, trying to relax his muscles. Ten minutes went by before he could get out of bed, then another fifteen to get dressed. He carried his boots downstairs with him. He could put them on after his muscles relaxed a little more.

Two dirty plates were stacked next to the sink. Ben was at the stove, cooking. Mack sat down at the table, next to Roy, as Ben poured him a mug of coffee. He set a plate of pancakes in front of him, then turned back to the stove. A thick T-bone steak, four eggs, hash browns, and biscuits made from a refrigerated tube of dough, followed the pancakes. Silence filled the kitchen while he ate.

It took Mack awhile to realize what was going on. When he did, he suppressed a smile. They were mothering him. Two tough old men were mothering him. Anyone who didn't know them well would never guess how gentle they could be. How, when they believed it was needed, they could so easily show their caring and concern.

Mack broke the quiet. "I've got to tell you," he said, tilting his chair back and pushing his empty plate away from him. "I haven't eaten anything so good since I won the bull ride at the Dallas rodeo."

"Been awhile then," Roy laughed, "since you ate good, hasn't it, Boy?"

"It has," Mack agreed, feeling a lot better. He was amazed at how much good could come from stuffing his gut.

Ben grinned, then looked Mack straight in the eye. "You have dreams that bad often, son?" he asked.

"Not always. That was the worst one I've had in a couple months."

"Need to talk about it?"

"Not just now."

"You ever need to, I'll listen."

"Yeah, I know," Mack answered, his voice choking. They were kind enough not to notice.

"I'd guess," Roy said, pushing away from the table, "it's time we whipped into it."

"I think you're right," Ben agreed. "Mind washing the dishes, Mack?"

"No, not a bit."

They left the house, and Mack started on the dishes, happy to have something simple to keep his hands busy. He kept his mind occupied by listening to a talk show on the radio. WCCO's favorite conservative talk show host was on, telling his audience about the Republicans' great plans for everyone. About how they and their ways were going to save the world from the evil federal government, which of course, the Republicans were now running. Nothing took Mack out of himself as quickly as listening to a conservative lie.

As far as he was concerned, the only thing any conservative ever cared about was the money lining some billionaire's pockets. Nothing else. They certainly wouldn't save anybody anything by giving the very rich more tax cuts. They were never willing to put money into schools, infrastructure, or the environment, all of which desperately needed it.

The environment and Republicans. Now there was a cruel joke. They'd probably rip up the National Forests again, the way they did at every opportunity. Build miles and miles of roads through the National Forests to make it easier for the big rich lumber companies to steal the trees. Not a dime more spent on the National Parks or Wildlife Refuges. Probably cut way back on them the same way they always did. Maybe sell them off, the fools. Yeah, maybe even sell them off. Maybe even…

I wonder, Mack thought, *I really wonder if they could do that? Maybe! They've sure screwed up more of the environment than most people realize. I think I'll go over to the refuge and see what I can find out.*

When he finished and was ready to leave, the phone rang. It was Jason.

"Mack," he said, "how are you doing?"

"Fine," Mack lied, "just fine."

"Good, glad to hear it. Listen, I'm really busy, so I can't talk long. I called to see if you're available tonight. I know it's short notice, but Mandy says it's about the only night we're free for the next couple of weeks."

"No problem. Tonight is fine."

"Well good," Jason said, his voice deflating. "I'll see you tonight, say, six, six-thirty."

"I'll be there."

"Okay." Jason hung up abruptly, leaving Mack wondering why he called.

Mack knew Jason long enough to be sure, from the tone of his voice, he was hoping Mack would decline the offer. Mack, however, wasn't about to. He wanted the chance to talk to Jason to learn as much as possible about the big project he was involved in and anything else he could find out that was connected with Ben losing the farm. First, though, he was going to visit the refuge.

It was a six-mile drive from Ben's farm to the refuge headquarters. Mack used the time to clear his head of everything, except the questions he wanted to ask. By the time he got there, he was so tightly wound, he found it necessary to stop and take a couple of deep breaths to calm down before he went inside. He was certain he'd learn more under the pretext of a social call than he would if he started off with a barrage of questions.

Inside, a woman whose nametag said Elaine, who wasn't there when Mack was a volunteer worker, sat at the front desk.

"Hi," he said, smiling. "Is Ray around?"

"Who?" she asked, looking up at him. She did a slight double take when she saw his face. Mack barely noticed.

"Ray Foss. He's still the manager here, isn't he?"

"No." Her initial sour look faded into something more akin to stone.

"Did he finally get the transfer he always talked about?"

"No. He died." She avoided eye contact. "Is there someone else you'd like to see?"

"No one in particular. I grew up not far from here. A farm on the south leg. I've been away more than five years. Before I left, I did volunteer work. I got back a few days ago and thought I'd stop in and say hello. Anyone still here who was around back then?"

"Two I can think of," she answered, her voice cold as ice. "There's Rich, of course. He'll never transfer. And Jerry's still here."

Mack was staring hard at her because of her reactions and noticed a bruise on her face, under her heavy makeup. It made him wonder whether she walked into cabinet doors or if she was a mugger like the one who attacked him the day he got out of the hospital.

"Either one of them around?" he asked, smiling this time at his own thoughts.

"Rich is out in the field." She frowned. "Over in the south leg working on some kind of impact study or something. Jerry's in his office, playing on the computer."

"Mind asking Jerry if it's okay for me to go in and say hello? I think he'll remember me. I'm Mack Thomas."

She attempted a smile. "I'll go ask him." Her frown won. She went into Jerry's office and was still frowning when she returned. "He said to go in," she said, then turned her back on him.

Jerry stood and greeted Mack with a wide smile and firm handshake when he entered the office. "How you been, guy?"

"Good, Jerry. You?"

"Real good. They haven't wised up enough to make me manager yet, but I keep hoping."

"You think they will? I thought they promoted the administrative types, not the biologists."

"I still keep hoping they'll wise up. What brings you over here after all this time?"

"I got back home a couple of days ago. Thought I'd stop and say hello. Too bad about Ray. What happened?"

"He shot himself."

"No kidding? Not Ray. He always seemed so in control."

"I guess he wasn't."

"How are things around here otherwise, now that the idiot Republicans have control again? They cut your budget to the bones yet?"

Jerry smiled. "You haven't changed."

"No, not much. Unlike you, I don't work for the federal government, so I can still call an idiot an idiot."

"I guess you can, Mack, if you have a mind to."

"Does it bother you? Never used to."

"I guess I'm just a little more cautious than I once was."

"What's there to be cautious about? Nothing I say will have any effect on you."

"Maybe not, then again…"

"Are you trying to get mysterious on me, Jerry?"

"That's a funny word, mysterious." His grin turned to a frown. "I don't think that's quite what I'm doing. How's your dad? I hear he's selling out."

"He's okay. And yes, he's selling out."

"Why?"

"He's broke. Lost his crops two years running."

"And he's such a good farmer. At least, you always said he was."

"He is."

"Then you've got a real mystery to solve, haven't you? A lot more than anything I could give you."

"Maybe, unless this refuge, or part of it anyway, is really going to be sold off and turned into some kind of resort?"

"It's been good seeing you, Mack. Stop in again."

"Are you telling me it's time for me to go?"

"Sure am. I've got a lot of reports to get out in the next couple of days, and like always, they were due yesterday."

"Okay. Take it easy, Jerry."

"You too, Mack."

Mack decided to take a different route home when he left the refuge headquarters, hoping he might find Rich. He turned west on the gravel county road, crossed the St. Catherine River on an ancient one-lane bridge, then drove a complete circuit around the refuge. As he neared home on the west side of the river, almost directly across it from Ben's farm, he noticed an open gate and drove in. A refuge pickup was parked about a quarter mile inside.

Mack stopped next to it and got out. Fresh tracks in the soft sand pointed toward the river, so he followed them. He found Rich sitting on a downed tree next to the river, holding a clipboard in one hand, tossing pebbles into the water with the other.

"Rich," he said, "how are you?"

"Same as always, Mack. You?"

"Fair."

"What brings you here? It's been years."

"I've been gone a long time. I always missed this place, so I thought I'd get reacquainted."

"Where you been?"

"Rodeo."

"Riding those crazy horses you always liked so much?"

"No, bulls mostly."

"You are a glutton for hurt."

"What're you up to? Back at the office they said you were doing some kind of impact study. You studying the impact of stones on water?"

"Just killing time, mostly."

"Why, your study isn't important?"

"Depends on how you look at it."

"What are you supposed to be studying?"

"There you go, Mack, asking questions about things I'm not supposed to give you the answers to. You want to get me in trouble?"

"No, I was just curious."

"It would be better for me if you weren't."

"Why, are all the rumors true? Is there something going on with the refuge the powers that be don't want us ordinary folk to know about?"

"Who've you been talking to, Mack?"

"Just people here and there."

"Just people, huh? I know you better than that."

"Tell me anyway, what the hell's going on."

"I can't. Not now."

"Okay, but does it have anything to do with Ray shooting himself?"

Rich responded with a sharp look. "You remember don't you, Mack, that Ray and I were good friends?"

"Yes, and it was a stupid question and none of my business. I'm sorry I asked."

"I don't mind your asking. You knew Ray pretty good too. Why are you so quick to believe he killed himself?"

"I have to admit, it doesn't sound like something he'd do."

"It wasn't. You also got to wonder why his family moved back to Colorado within two weeks. The Fish and Wildlife Service not only paid the whole moving bill, they also bought them a house, then handled the sale of Ray's house here."

"You saying you think Ray didn't shoot himself?"

"I'm not saying anything."

"You could have fooled me."

"I don't think I could do that, Mack." Rich smiled. "Sure is a pretty spot here," he said, changing the subject. "Probably the prettiest spot in the refuge. It would be a real shame if someone built a dam downstream and flooded it."

"Okay, what's this flooding deal about?"

"Nothing, it'd just be a shame if it ever happened. Now I think you ought to haul yourself back home. We're supposed to keep everyone out of here you know."

"I know. It was good seeing you again, Rich. Be okay if I stop around again sometime?"

"Sure, so long as you're not full of questions."

"Okay."

Rich gave Mack a lot to think about. More questions than answers.

Chapter 11

Mack went back to painting and repairing outbuildings. He was up high, working on the back end of the barn, when a hole exploded in the barn siding, inches from his head. When he heard the gunshot, he was so startled, he jumped, knocking the bottom of the ladder loose from the ground. It slid straight out from the barn, and he rode it down the barn's wall.

Two more bullets hit the barn above his head before his ride down ended with a jolt. The ladder landed on soft ground, so he wasn't seriously hurt and was only left with a searing pain in his lower back.

Ben and Roy rushed out of the machine shed next to the barn, where they'd been repairing the old machinery for the coming auction.

"What the hell was that?" Roy asked.

Mack was trying hard not to groan.

"I think," he said, "that some fool on the other side of the river wasn't paying any attention to what he was shooting at. He hit the barn about two inches from my head. It scared the hell out of me, and when I jumped, the ladder broke loose. Felt like I was back in rodeo when it landed."

Roy stared up at the barn. "It's probably a good thing it did slide, Mack. If you'd of stayed there, my guess is you'd be real bad hurt right now. Maybe even dead."

"You look to be hurting anyway, Mack," Ben said. "You going to be okay? Maybe I ought to run you into the hospital, make sure there's nothing broke."

"I'm okay, Dad. If I wasn't hurting already, I wouldn't have hit hard enough to matter. The pain was already there. It's just worse now."

"I don't like this one bit. Let's go inside for a while, have some coffee, and talk about it."

"Sure, Dad."

"Good idea," Roy agreed.

"I'm wondering," Ben said when they were all sitting at the table with mugs of coffee in front of them, "if maybe we should call the sheriff?"

"I don't think there's much the sheriff could do, Dad," Mack said. "The odds are it was a poacher doing the shooting, so it's highly unlikely that he will hang around long."

"What about the wildlife people?"

"I doubt they'll be able to do anything, either, but if it'll make you feel any better, I can give them a call."

"It would, so do it."

Mack called and talked to Elaine. She told him she'd try to get someone to check it out. They talked about the shooting for a while after he made the call. Their conversation gradually drifted onto other topics, and less than an hour later, they were out working again. Mack stayed on the ground, moving slowly the rest of the day.

While he worked, he ran the questions bothering him through his head. Exactly where was the bank's big project going to be built? From what he'd learned, it'd be on and around the south leg of the refuge, with a dam large enough to create a lake inside the high banks of the river. If they needed a lake, it confirmed Mandy's comment about the project, leaving little doubt it would be a resort of some kind. Driving around earlier, it was obvious that both sides of the refuge's south leg had been bought up and the people who lived there moved off. Ben's eighty acres was the largest place left and sat in the middle of the east side, bordering a quarter mile of the refuge, so it was easy to see why the bank wanted the ground. The farm was definitely in the way.

Another question was Ben's crops. What was killing them? The damage looked to Mack like herbicide poisoning. Damage to the crops in the past, from other farmers' herbicide overspray, was minor and only on the edges of the fields. So if the damage to the crops was caused by herbicides, it was unlikely that it was caused accidentally.

The death of Ray Foss, the former refuge manager, was also a question. How did he die if it wasn't suicide? Who'd murder him, why was he murdered, and how did they make it look so much like suicide? Was he killed only because he didn't want part of the refuge sold? It didn't seem to be enough motive for murder.

That brought up another question. Were those rifle shots really an accident, as he'd tried to assure Ben and Roy they were? It seemed probable that they were, the same as the attempted mugging right after he left the hospital was a coincidence. A lot had happened to him since coming home, and he'd seen two people with bruises on their faces, much like the one he was sure he'd left on the mugger's face? He didn't believe they were muggers, but it was interesting.

Whether or not any of what happened was connected to the project or simply a coincidence, Mack no longer doubted someone worked out a deal to buy the south leg of the refuge. Selling part of a wildlife refuge was minor, compared to what he knew could be expected from mindless Republicans. The resort wouldn't only be using part of the refuge, it'd be destroying an even larger part of it. Building a dam to flood the south leg also meant they'd be flooding much of the remaining refuge. Apparently, no one involved cared how much damage would be done.

With all the questions he had, Mack was anxious to get to Jason's that evening, hoping he would find some answers.

Mandy answered the door when he got there a little early. She was wearing an old pair of loose-fitting jeans and an even looser sweat-shirt. She still wore her daytime makeup, and her hair was freshly combed. She gave Mack a small smile and a weak hello, then escorted him into the living room. Jason was sitting in an easy chair, engrossed in the financial section from the *Minneapolis Star Tribune*. He finished what he was reading before he acknowledged Mack's presence.

He was still wearing his banker's suit, although he had loosened his tie. When he finally set the paper on an end table, his greeting to Mack was a short wave of the hand, motioning for him to sit down.

"So," Mack asked, hoping to start a conversation, "how's it going?"

"So, so. This heat is really getting to me."

Mack smiled, wishing he could answer Jason's ridiculous comment. Jason's home and office were air conditioned, and it was likely his car was too. How could the heat be bothering him?

"The heat's not so bad," Mack said finally.

"Not so bad? It's awful. The electric bill has been incredible."

"Turn off the air conditioner or at least turn it down."

"I can't do that living here in town. Out in the country, you get a breeze. We don't."

"There hasn't been much of a breeze anywhere the past few days. It's still not so bad."

"I have to be presentable at my job. I can't go around full of sweat and wearing wrinkled clothes."

"I guess not."

"There's no guessing, Mack. If you'd ever had a real job or taken any kind of responsibility in your life, you'd know it."

"You bet, if you say so, Jason."

"If I say so. You know damn well you've…"

"Jason!" Mack said loud enough to make Jason jump. "If you're planning on giving me one of your lectures, forget it. I'm not in the mood for it tonight. The fact is, I don't always approve of the way you do things, either."

"What do you mean by that?"

"Exactly what I said. Maybe I haven't done any great things with my life, but I haven't taken part in throwing people off their land. Any money I've ever had, I worked hard for. I didn't get it by sitting on my fat ass in an air-conditioned office."

"If that's your attitude, you can leave my house right now!"

"That's fine by me." Mack stood to leave.

"No way, Mack!" Mandy said, entering the room. "You're not going anywhere."

Mack felt like a fool standing there, looking into Mandy's eyes, which were pleading with him to stay. They convinced him to swallow his pride. Nothing else could make him stay. Only the look in her eyes. He sat back down.

"Jason," Mandy said, "you invited Mack for supper tonight, not me. So at least be civil until he's eaten."

"Yes, you're right, honey. I'm sorry, Mack, I guess I got carried away. I've been tired and edgy lately from the long hours I work and this awful heat."

"Forget it," Mack said, trying to sound unconcerned. "Why are you working so hard?"

"The usual stuff. There's been a lot of extra paperwork to do to get the bank transferred over to the new owners, merging the accounts from all the banks involved. That's in addition to the work I've always done." He didn't mention his special project.

Mack wanted to press him but couldn't on the chance Jason might guess that he heard about the project from Mandy. So the conversation stopped until Mandy sat them down to eat. They ate a simple country meal of roast chicken, mashed potatoes, homemade gravy, and cream-style corn. It was delicious, and Mack said so.

"Thank you, Mack," she said, "it's nice to get a compliment on my cooking. Even from you."

"What's that supposed to mean?" Jason growled.

"Only that a compliment from Mack on my or anyone's cooking is rather easy to get. Have you forgotten what an appetite he's always had?"

"I never gave it any thought. But it doesn't surprise me you would."

"It's only natural she'd notice, Jason," Mack said. "She's the one who did the cooking. Julie used to say the same thing about me."

"Mandy's not your wife."

"Neither is Julie. She's dead, remember?" Mack gritted his teeth, trying not to lose his temper.

"It must have been hard for you when she died," Mandy said, sensing Mack's mood and hoping to keep the two men away from each other's throats. "I mean, with you being alone and so far from home and all."

"I think it was a lot harder on her, Mandy."

"I didn't mean it that way."

"I know, but if I'd have stayed with her that night instead of insisting I ride in the next rodeo, she'd probably still be alive."

"Why do you blame yourself? It's terrible she had an accident, but that's what it was."

"What makes you think you know so much about it, Mandy?" Jason said. "Maybe it was his fault?"

"It was more than an accident," Mack said. "We had a fight about my riding in the next rodeo. It was small, not much prize money in it." He paused, wondering why he was telling Mandy about it. It was something he'd never told anyone. "She wanted me to skip it, to give us a chance to rest after the heavy schedule we were following. It was the worst fight we ever had. I was too stubborn to give in and mad as hell when I left her. She was too. I hitched a ride with another cowboy, Jimmy Rail, and left the pickup with her. I guess after a while, she decided to come. It was late by then. She fell asleep doing about ninety miles an hour and rolled the truck at the bottom of a long hill without the seat belt on. They kept her coffin closed at the funeral."

"You two are morbid," Jason said, leaving the table. He stood for a moment, then gave Mack the rest of his opinion. "If you had God in your heart, Mack, you wouldn't be dwelling on her. You were simply his instrument when you caused her death."

He left the room.

"That's exactly what I needed," Mack said, turning to Mandy.

Tears rolled down her cheeks. She reached out and took his hand and their eyes met. Her grip was strong, and Mack knew instantly that she still felt the same as he did. She'd only buried the feelings deeper than he had.

Mandy was the first to turn away, dropping her hand in her lap as she did. Mack pushed away from the table, touched her cheek to brush away a tear, then left the house.

"So much for learning something," he said to himself on the way to Roy's truck.

CHAPTER 12

It was early in the evening, still daylight, and Mack was in no mood to go back to the farm. He drove out in the country, randomly following different roads, eventually stopping at a country bar typical of those frequently found on Minnesota's back roads. It served three-two beer, burgers, French fries, and nothing else. It was located on a slight curve in the road and was named The Mystic Curve Inn. Most people simply called it The Curve.

Inside, he sat down at the bar, put his elbows on its plastic top, ordered a glass of tap beer, and looked around. It was a small place. Several wobbly tables with uncomfortable chairs filled most of the floor space, a few booths ran along one wall, and a dusty pool table sat unused near the back. The only other customers in the place were two old couples playing cards at one of the tables.

His first beer tasted good and the quiet was pleasant, so he bought a pitcher of beer and carried it over to a booth. He was on his second glass when he got company. She'd been drinking before she got there. It showed when she sat down and filled her glass from his pitcher. She gulped the beer down and filled her glass again before saying anything.

"Hi there, Mack," she said, her words slurred. "Remember me?"

He did, vaguely. He couldn't remember her name and he admitted it.

"It's because I've been away for a long time," he explained.

"Name's Wanda. Wanda Peterson. We were in high school together. Graduated the same time."

Even though she jogged his memory, he barely remembered her. Jason was the only real friend he had during his high school years. He spent very little time with any of the rest of his peer group. Most of the time, he was helping Ben work the farm, riding his horse, exploring the refuge, and when he felt like it, studying.

"Yeah, I remember you, we were in the same English class or something?"

"That's right," she grinned, "in our junior year. In our freshman year, we were in social studies…"

She delivered a litany of all the classes they'd been in together through several years of school. He pretended to listen to her while concentrating on getting the bartender's attention. They had a second pitcher in front of them before she completed her list. She did most of the talking while they drank. When the beer was gone, Mack was ready to leave and said so.

"Oh, come on, Mack," she whined, "don't be in such a hurry. It's kind of fun, isn't it, talking about old times?"

"I guess, but I have to get up early."

"Well," she grinned, "if you don't want to stay here, follow me home. I've got some beer there," her grin widened, "and a king-size bed."

Mack looked at her without answering. She was more than pretty enough, so it was a tempting offer. But she'd had too much to drink. If he accepted her invitation, there would be too many questions in the morning. Sober, she'd likely look at it very differently than she did now. He gave her a polite no thank you and left.

She followed him out, then flew past him on the county road. A few miles later, there was a rainbow of flashing lights at the side of the road. Mack stopped behind the sheriff's car as the deputy was trying to put Wanda in the back seat.

"Hello, Mack," the deputy said as Mack walked up to him. He was another high school acquaintance.

"Hi," Mack answered, then paused, trying to remember his name. "You're Dale Magee, aren't you?" he said when he finally remembered. "How's it going?"

"Fine. What can I do for you? I know you didn't stop to chat."

"No, I didn't know it was you when I stopped. Didn't even know you were a cop. Wanda's the reason for stopping. I was with her for a while at the bar back there."

Wanda picked up her drooping head and glared at him "No, you weren't. We were at the same bar is all. I wouldn't ever be any-place with you."

"I feel responsible for this happening, Dale," he said, ignoring Wanda. "I wonder if it would be okay for me to give her a lift home? I'd hate to see her spend the night in jail."

Dale grinned. "So would I. I'm not supposed to do anything like this, but what the hell. She's an okay person, she's just being stupid. I hate locking people up for bad judgment, when there's so many real criminals out and about who really need locking up and probably won't be."

"I ain't going with him," Wanda complained.

"Would you rather go to jail?" Dale asked.

"Jail? I thought you were going to take me home. I have a king-size bed, you know."

"Wanda, if you don't go with Mack, I'll have to take you to the county jail. I can't let you drive."

"I don't want him to take me home."

"Why not?"

"I just don't like him."

"The hell with it, Mack." Dale winked. "I guess Wanda wants to spend the night in jail."

"No, I don't," Wanda complained, her foggy brain finally grasping what was happening. "He can take me home. He just ain't staying."

Dale helped her into the truck. She slumped against the door. Dale drove her car farther off the road, then gave Mack the keys.

"This isn't something I'd normally do," Dale said. "The thing is, if you can handle those bulls I've heard you've been riding, you should be able to take care of one drunk female."

"I'll do my best. How'd you know I've been riding bulls?"

"I saw your name in a rodeo newsletter when the rodeo was here in an article about bull riding. You were mentioned because you're local." Dale took one of his cards out of a pocket, turned it over, and wrote his home phone number on it. "Give me a call sometime, Mack," he said, handing it to him. "We'll go have a beer or something."

"Sure, I'd like that."

"Take care now."

He left and Mack took Wanda home. She passed out before they got to town, so he stopped to dig her driver's license out of her purse to find her address. She lived in an apartment above a store on Kingsburg's main street. To avoid any questions from her neighbors, he parked in back and carried her up to her apartment.

He dropped her on her king-size bed and covered her with a blanket, then stretched out on her couch in the living room. He wanted to leave and would have, if he hadn't been so worried she'd get herself into trouble if she woke up while she was still drunk. He felt he'd already let her down by letting her drive and didn't want to fail her again. After what happened to Julie, his conscience bothered him enough.

He woke up with the first daylight, used the bathroom, then looked in on her. She was huddled on the corner of the bed, the blanket clutched around her, her eyes filled with terror.

"Mack," she said, relaxing as soon as she saw him, "what are you doing here?"

"I took you home last night."

"Now I remember. I had a beer with you. I don't remember anything else, though." She got out of bed, holding her head. "Oh my god, what a headache."

"Too much beer can do that to you."

"I know," she said, clutching her stomach and running for the bathroom.

He waited for her in the living room. A while later, she joined him, her face pale and her hands shaking.

"Thank you," she said, "for taking me home. More than that, thank you for not taking advantage of the situation. Why are you still here?"

"To keep you out of trouble. I figured you'd had enough for one night."

"What do you mean?"

He told her about the night's events, and although she was embarrassed enough to blush, she managed to laugh.

"I don't suppose I could impose on you again and ask you to give me a ride out to my car?"

"No problem, if you'll fix me a cup of coffee first?"

"Instant okay? It's all I've got."

"Anything, so long as it's hot and black."

Wanda didn't talk as much as she did the night before. By the time Mack finished his coffee though, they knew each other a little better. They agreed to get together later in the week when he drove her out to her car.

Chapter 13

As he entered the bar, Jason sucked in his gut to hide his slight paunch and threw back his shoulders to make the most of his otherwise slight five-foot ten-inch frame. It was something he made a habit of doing. He believed it was necessary to impress people as much with his stature as with his position, if they were to be controlled. He sat down with a brief nod to Elaine and the man with her.

"So," he asked immediately, "what's up that we needed this meeting?"

"Mack Thomas," Elaine said, "Ben Thomas's kid—"

Jason interrupted. "What about him?"

"He was at the refuge, asking a lot of questions. Jerry told him about Ray, and I think it got him real curious. We really should do something about him before he causes us a lot of trouble."

"We're done in that department. Ray was necessary because of the way he fought us so hard, trying to preserve the refuge for himself and the rest of the nature lovers. But there's no reason to have more of that kind of thing now."

"We have too much at stake in this deal, Jason," the man said, "to be taking chances. We can't let it get messed up from his nosing into it. He needs taking out, so the sooner we do it, the better."

"To start with, I make those decisions. I don't think we should. I hate the idiot, but now is not the time. We must be careful and not do anything to attract attention. Trying to kill him in some godforsaken rodeo town was one thing. Trying to fake anything with Mack while he's here is something else. His old man would never believe it no matter how good you made it look. If you get him and Mack's uncle looking into anything like that, we'll have some very serious problems. I'm not referring to legal crap, either."

"I have to tell you, Jason, if we let this ride and the kid learns too much before the corporation has the Thomas place, it could queer this whole deal. Too many people have too much invested to let it happen. You know how much I've put into it. You handled the money for me."

"You came by it easy enough, after I told you what to do to get it. So far, nothing's happened because of Mack. I can't see anything happening that we need to get excited about. The auction's coming up real soon, so it won't be long before the company owns the Thomas Place. Mack won't be able to do a thing about what he learns then."

"No, he won't," Elaine said, "unless he learns too much about Ray. When we tried to get rid of him a year ago, it was because you were worried he might come home and screw things up. Now that he's here, you've changed your mind. It doesn't make sense."

"But it does. We're a lot closer to finalizing the deal now. It doesn't matter what he finds out about Ray or anything else. It won't do him any good. Ray's family and the police believe the official version. Isn't that right?"

Jason looked at the man and he nodded yes. "Who's going to listen to a dumb cowboy? They'll think he banged his head too many times, falling off all those bulls."

"You better make sure it stays that way."

"I will, and I expect you two to stay calm. We can always consider other options later, if it's necessary."

"We're calm," the man said, standing to leave. He looked at Elaine. "You ready to go?"

She looked at her watch. "I haven't got much time before I have to be back. I'm going to finish my drink with Jason, then run."

"I guess it's okay this time, so long as you don't make a habit out of it. We'll be talking."

He left, then paused a moment before getting into his car, wondering if he should try once more to kill Mack Thomas. Although

Jason didn't know it, there'd been three attempts to kill him, and Mack somehow escaped every one of them. Was it worth trying a fourth time?

Inside the bar, Jason waited until the big man walked out, then said, "Aren't you worried he'll get jealous, Elaine? It might have been better to go with him."

"No," she smiled, "he's always jealous anyway. I can handle anything with him, one way or the other. Don't forget, it was you who told me I worked magic, and if I did it right, I'd be able to control him. Him and all the rest of the men you wanted handled, even if I don't enjoy doing it as much as I used to."

Jason frowned. "The fact that he's so stupid worries me. You never know what he's going to do if you don't keep tight control over him."

"Not a problem." She laughed. "I promise you, I know how to handle the fat slob. I'll keep him doing what you want done."

"I guess you will."

"Damn right, and there's no guessing. You know better than anyone how good the magic is."

"Sure I do, but you don't need to enjoy it. Not with them."

"I only enjoy the controlling part, making them do the things we need done and knowing we, and only we, will profit from it in the end. The other stuff is mostly only fun with you. I drove the van today. I've got enough time if you want to do it."

"Are you kidding? That's really pushing our luck. We're getting too close to completing the project to be taking any unnecessary chances."

"It makes it more exciting. I enjoy pushing the edge. That's why all this is so easy. There can be more to this than money, you know."

"Not for me. How about I knock off early today and meet you at the usual place?"

"I guess, if that's the best you can do. It'll have to be a quick one. My husband is expecting me to be home on time tonight, and he's one person we still really need."

"That's okay, a quick one will fit best with my schedule too."

"Sure, but nothing on your schedule can give you what I can. Not even money can give it to you."

Jason smiled, knowing he'd let her think whatever she wanted to, as long as he had a use for her.

Chapter 14

Mack continued to work around the farm, painting and repairing. Although he was certain none of what was going on was a coincidence, he hadn't figured out what his next step should be.

Ben and Roy were still putting their efforts into cleaning and repairing machinery, and the three of them spent their evenings outside in the shade of the oak tree, drinking beer and talking. It was always dark before it was cool enough to go inside.

They were eating dinner, two days after Mack ate supper at Jason's, when Mandy caught Mack near the phone. He answered it when it rang.

"Is that you, Mack?" she asked.

"It is," he said, happy to hear her voice, his heart thumping with excitement.

"Good. I didn't want to get your dad or Roy."

"They won't bite, you know."

"I know, it's just easier for me this way. I'm on my lunch break so I can't talk long. I was wondering if you're free tomorrow? I have the day off. I'd like to see…well, talk to you, if you have time?"

"Of course I have time. When and where?"

"The morning's best. I'd like to go someplace where there aren't people around. I don't think I should be seen with you. Jason's going to Saint Paul tomorrow for an early meeting with the bank's new owners, so he won't know what I'm doing."

"How about meeting in the wildlife refuge? At the old schoolhouse, where the hiking trail starts. It isn't likely we'll see anyone there, as hot as it is."

"Sounds good. What time?"

"Six."

"In the morning?"

"It's the best time of the day to spend there, Mandy."

"Okay, I'll be there."

Mack didn't volunteer anything about the conversation when he went back to the table, and Ben and Roy were polite enough not to ask. Mack worked the rest of the afternoon, filled with a tense, uneasy feeling. He wasn't sure what caused it and couldn't shake it by working. So he quit early, and hoping that getting out and stretching his legs would help get rid of the feeling, he walked to the refuge again. He followed a different trail this time, and it took him across a wide, shallow spot in the river. After climbing the riverbank, he crossed a seldom-used maintenance road and followed it north.

As he reached a bend in the road, he heard voices. Not anyone talking, only a lot of ohs and ahs and high pitched guttural sounds. Someone was either being murdered or making love. He left the road, having no desire to interfere with anyone's love life. He felt though, that he should stay and find out what was going on, just in case.

Trying to be as quiet as possible, he crept through the underbrush until he was in sight of a late-model car and a refuge van. Suddenly, there was a scream. Before he could react to it, the two voices settled into a steady stream of "oh-oh-oh." It was obvious no one was being murdered, so he decided to leave whoever it was alone and finish his walk in the other direction. A second look at the car stopped him. It looked familiar. Too familiar. Like the car parked in Jason's driveway the night Mack visited him. Who's in the van, he wondered? He waited to find out.

Only moments later, the rear doors opened. Jason was the first one out, followed by Elaine, the woman Mack talked to at the refuge headquarters. Jason was tucking his shirt into his pants. She was out before putting on her bra. She asked Jason to hook it for her, which he did, after fondling her ample breasts. Then she put on the top half of her refuge uniform.

"This isn't enough anymore," she said to Jason, "As soon as the project construction is started, you're going to make the changes. I want to get back to Washington as soon as possible."

"Don't try to rush me, Elaine. I've got a lot of responsibilities to take care of, and I don't like it when you push."

"Listen," she yelled, "after all I've done for you, I'll push you all I want. You really owe me now, just as much as you need what I give you. I know your prissy wife doesn't give you what I do. No other woman does or can."

Jason slapped her hard across her face. Startled from the blow, she hesitated, then moved her hand to her cheek and touched the red mark his blow left there. "You son of a bitch!"

"That's right," Jason agreed, "and you'll get worse if you ever threaten me again. I can be as violent as you are, if I have to be." He turned and walked toward his car.

She jumped after him, grabbing his arm. "Now you wait a…"

Jason knocked her down. She was back on her feet in an instant, then buried her right hand deep into his gut. He doubled over.

"You better learn now, Jason, not to try knocking me around. I won't take it like your little wifey does!"

Jason merely stood there, making loud sucking sounds as he tried to get his breath back.

"You better know I feel the same, bitch," he gasped after he was breathing again, then got in his car and drove away.

She picked up a rock and threw it at the car, bouncing it off a fender.

"Damn you!" she screamed at the retreating car. "You bastard!"

Tears streamed down her face, even though her expression was more of anger than anything. "He's lucky," she said aloud to herself, "I love him so much. If I didn't, I'd kill him."

Mack watched her brush herself off before she drove away. It wasn't until he was almost back to the farm that he remembered the bruise on Mandy's face. He carried that picture of her in his head the rest of the way home.

Ben and Roy were eating when he went inside the house.

"Food's on the stove," Ben said. "Help yourself."

Mack filled his plate with the hash in the frying pan, then topped it with a couple of fried eggs on a warming plate.

"Have a nice walk?" Roy asked.

"Yes and no."

"What's that mean?"

"The walk was good, what I saw wasn't."

"What was it you saw?"

"I ran across Jason, poking one of the refuge ladies in her van."

"It happens, Mack. He isn't the first man to cheat on his wife."

"I know and I could care less. It was when he tried to knock her around that bothers me."

"He did it with you there?"

"I stayed in the brush. I didn't know it was him when I walked up on them, and I'd have gotten out of there if the noise they made didn't sound as much like murder as lovemaking. When they got out of the van, she said something about the big project we keep hearing about, so I stayed to see if I'd learn anything. Next thing I know, he's knocking her around and she's fighting back. It's hard to say who got the best of it."

"Maybe she'll know better next time and stay away from him."

"I was thinking about Mandy. I'm sure Jason's been abusing her."

"What makes you think so?" Roy asked, without showing any surprise.

"When she was here the other day, she had a bruise on her cheek. It didn't come from any cabinet door like she said it did. I'm sure now that Jason gave it to her. The woman he was with tonight said something about not taking anything from him the way his wife does. The other day when I stopped at the refuge, I saw a bruise on her cheek too."

"You're probably right on both counts, Mack," Ben said. "Still, there isn't much you can do about it. It's not right to be messing around in another man's marriage."

"I don't agree with you, Dad. If he's beating her, I'd be wrong not to. Letting him do it isn't right."

"I guess I have to admit to that. Especially when you care about someone, the way I'm sure you still care about Mandy. What're you planning to do?"

"I'm seeing Mandy tomorrow. I'll talk to her about it before I do anything."

"We thought you were going to see her," Roy said.

"I can't say either one of us thinks it's a good idea," Ben added, "but you're old enough to make your own decisions. Just be careful you don't get yourself into something you don't want to be into."

"I will. And when I'm talking to her, I'll see if she knows anything more about the project."

"What for?" Ben asked. "Won't save this farm, no matter what you learn. It's too late now."

"Maybe, maybe not. Either way, I want to know what it's all about."

Chapter 15

Mack was up and out of the house before the first light of morning, taking a small pack of food, water, and a bottle of red wine with him. It was a cool morning, a welcome relief from the heat, which had been constant since the day he got home.

He walked to the schoolhouse where he was planning to meet Mandy. He ignored the refuge rules and traveled cross-country, using maintenance roads, then animal trails when they made the walk shorter. He thought he'd get there well ahead of her because he was early and knew she had a habit of being late, so it was pleasant surprise to see her car when he arrived.

"It's beautiful, isn't it?" Mandy said, getting out of the car and pointing to a few wispy clouds on the eastern horizon, glowing red in the early morning sun.

"It is," Mack agreed, then carelessly said, "like you."

She blushed, smiled, then quickly changed the subject. "I rarely get to see the sun come up."

"I rarely get to spend the day with a beautiful woman," Mack countered, wanting her to acknowledge his compliment.

"You're easier and quicker with your compliments, Mack, than you used to be. Did you get a lot of practice while you were a rodeo cowboy?"

"No, I'm just not as shy as I used to be. You get over it when one bull or another is forever dumping you on your ass in front of several hundred people."

"I suppose that might do it."

He caught her eyes, and she quickly turned away, staring at her foot, nervously pushing loose sand around. He wanted to tell her how he felt but knew it wouldn't be a good idea. He took her hand and led her down the narrow trail.

They didn't talk right away, and the silence between them seemed natural. Mack picked up on the life sounds around them, first the insect hum, then birds singing and squirrels chattering in the trees. Cresting a small hill, they surprised a small herd of white-tail deer. He counted nine white flags as they raised their tails while running for cover.

"Wow," Mandy said after they disappeared, "I didn't know there were so many deer here."

"I've seen herds of twenty-five or more. That's part of why I like to get here early. There's more activity among the critters now than there will be later."

"I guess I forgot how nice this place is. I haven't been here since the last time you took me."

"That was a long time ago. Doesn't Jason ever bring you here?"

"Jason doesn't take me anywhere, except to dinners or parties that are connected to his work."

"Somehow, that doesn't surprise me."

She didn't comment on Jason any further, so he turned his attention back to their surroundings.

They were walking through an area of oak savannah, with a stand of oaks about a hundred yards to their right and running for a half mile ahead of them. Watching the trees against the horizon, he sensed something moving on the ground outside the stand of trees. He pointed out a coyote for Mandy. It took her a while before she managed to see it just as it disappeared into the woods.

"Why did you see it?" she asked. "I was looking over there before you pointed to it. I couldn't see anything other than trees and grass."

"I've had a lot of practice, watching for animals out here."

An eagle soared in from the west and landed in a high tree at the edge of a pond. They stopped to watch it. When it flew off, Mack turned his attention to Mandy. It was difficult not to take her in his arms, kiss her, and ask her a million questions.

"Well," he said, using words to hold in his feelings, "you said yesterday you wanted to talk to me."

"Now that I've got you here, Mack, I don't know how to start. Or even if you want to hear what I was going to say."

"The best way to find out is to just say it."

"Life is always so simple to you, Mack. This isn't."

"What's so complicated? We haven't seen or talked to each other in years, so it doesn't matter what you say. It isn't going to put any holds or ties on you."

"Hasn't it occurred to you, Mack, that I might want to put some on you?"

"No."

"I'd better not say anything then."

"Why not? I just couldn't ever make myself believe you would."

"You were wrong."

"I can't tell you how happy I am to hear that. But before we go any farther with this, I've got to ask you a question. Why all the makeup?"

"I always wear makeup."

"You didn't used to."

"I was younger then."

"What's the real reason you wore makeup today?"

"I wanted to look nice."

"You'd look good no matter what you did. What I really want to know is how did you get the bruise on your cheek and now the mark under your eye?"

"Mack, please, it's nothing."

"It's not nothing. Jason did it, didn't he?"

"Please don't do this. I've only seen you get angry once, and it scared the hell out of me. Forget about this, please."

"I can't, and you know it."

"You're so stubborn all the time."

"I know I'm stubborn. I care too. What he's doing to you isn't right."

"Forget about it, Mack. I can handle it."

"How? By taking more beatings? That's not handling it, Mandy. That's only being stupid."

"Mack, please don't…"

Mandy dropped her head in her hands and cried. He held her the way he'd longed to, until she stopped shaking and melted against him. She slowly lifted her head, then wrapped her arms around his neck, and kissed him.

"Damn you, Mack Thomas," she said, pushing away from him, "for needing to be who you are. Why did you have to go away and ride bulls? You should've stayed here with me."

"If I wouldn't have gone, if I'd have stayed here with you, then you would hate me. I'd hate me. It wouldn't have worked. Back then, I couldn't live locked up in some office. I still can't."

"I know, but why'd you have to be so filled with ideals and wanderlust and dreams and needing to prove something no one else cared about?"

"You mean, don't you, why wasn't I more like Jason?"

"No. I wouldn't want you to be like him. I wouldn't want anyone to be like him. Why couldn't you be a little more normal though? Why was it so important for you to ride bulls?"

"I guess it's because there's more to it than riding bulls. All my life, most of what I was told in school, church, by friends and acquaintances, and even sometimes by Dad, was what I couldn't do. I knew I could ride pretty good and thought it might be fun to try riding rodeo. I might not have done it if anyone else except Roy would've said it was okay to go ahead and try. No one did. I rode bulls because they were bigger, meaner, and harder to ride than horses."

"Maybe you would've won more if you rode horses."

"I'd never have been a champion anyway. I knew that before I started. The crap kids get fed about how they've got to be the best, number one, or it isn't worth doing is not only a lie of the biggest order, it's very unfair. How can everyone be number one? All I wanted was the chance to ride. Win or lose didn't matter so much as giving it my best shot."

"You didn't get much for it, did you?"

"I got more than most people ever get out of life. Five years of doing exactly what I wanted to do. It taught me that it's okay to set my own goals. There's a lot more to life than chasing money, the way Jason's done."

"So what are you going to do with your life now that you proved your point? There are a lot of things you could've done that you can't do now."

"Because of the experience, there are things I can do now I'd never be able to if I hadn't gone. In time, I'll figure out what they are."

"Don't you have any regrets?"

"Sure. I'm reminded of them every time I look at you. The past is past though, Mandy, and it can't be changed. So I don't want to spend a lot of time dwelling on it."

"I understand. If I disagreed with you, I think I'd hate you for running off the way you did."

"As it is, I don't think I'd blame you. If I could be more normal, I think we would've had a pretty good life together."

"It wasn't you who was wrong, Mack. It was me. I know that now. The right thing for me to do back then was to go with you, not to expect you to change who you are and stay with me. I didn't have dreams, only fear. Fear of what I didn't understand. Worse than that, fear of not having the things I thought I should have. Things that mean so little now."

"How'd you come to that conclusion so suddenly?"

"It wasn't sudden. I've suspected it for years. I simply confirmed it today."

"How's that?"

"Today made me realize I still love you as much as I ever did. Whatever it is you do now, wherever you go, I want to share it with you."

"Be damned," Mack said, then kissed her.

"That's why," she said, "I don't want you to get angry with Jason. I'll handle it and I'll soon be out of his life. I just need a little time."

"Okay, but..."

"No buts," she said, putting her hand over his mouth, "and no trouble. A little time and we'll be together."

Mack nodded in agreement, while wishing the tightness in his gut wasn't there, and that he could be sure time was the only thing they needed.

Chapter 16

Ben and Roy were working on the tractor when Mack got back to the farm. He waved at them, then went into the house and put his pack away. He was in the kitchen, drinking a second mug of coffee when they joined him.

"How's the refuge?" Roy asked, pouring himself and Ben a mug of coffee.

"Beautiful, like always."

"How's Mandy? You two solve anything?"

"I don't know. Maybe. She admitted Jason's been abusing her. Said she plans on leaving him."

"When?"

"I'm not sure. She said she needs a little more time."

"That all she said?"

"No. She said she loves me and wants us to spend the rest of our lives together. Even if I'm not put into a harness."

"Well, Mack," Ben said, "none of this is what you'd call a big surprise to me. Roy either. Are you sure you know what you're getting yourself into?"

"Some I do, some I don't."

"What's the part you don't know?"

"What to do about Jason. It scares me that she's still living with him. She told me, though, that she didn't want me to make any trouble."

"You aren't going to, are you?"

"Not as long as he doesn't hurt her."

"I understand how you feel. If he does anything, just get her the hell out of there."

"I don't want any trouble. Just don't ever ask me to run from it if it comes."

"Never would. Only that you don't go looking for it."

"I won't. Why aren't you two giving me royal hell about Mandy? You both taught me it isn't ever right to mess with another man's woman."

"'Cause it's a fact," Roy answered, "even if a thing is wrong most of the time, it doesn't mean it's wrong all the time. Given everything involved in this situation, I don't guess we could be sitting in any kind of judgment. Our only concern is that you don't get messed up by it."

"I won't be."

"Good," Ben said. "Well, Roy, I guess we best get back to it."

They left the house. Mack drank another mug of coffee before going to work himself.

His thoughts continually drifted back to Mandy. By late afternoon, he was thinking of nothing else. Because he knew Jason wasn't supposed to be home, he went inside and called her. Jason, who'd intentionally gotten home earlier than he said he would, answered the phone. Mack hung up immediately, knowing any conversation with him would be clumsy at best.

It bothered Mack when he didn't talk to her. Since there was nothing he could do about it, he decided to call her at her office the next day, hoping they could decide on the next step then.

It still worried him, so the call he received right after supper was welcome. It was Wanda.

"Hi, Mack," she said. "I called to see if you're free tonight."

"Sure."

"Would you like to go out and have something to eat with me and maybe a couple of beers?"

"I already ate. But I'd be glad to meet you for a couple of beers."

"Okay. Do you like music?"

"If you mean the usual bar music like rock and roll, no. Country might be okay, but I'd rather go to some place quiet. How about The Curve where we were the other night?"

"Okay. I'll pick you up, and we can ride out there together."

"That isn't necessary."

"I don't mind, and this way, you won't need to borrow your uncle's truck."

"What the hell, sure, pick me up."

He didn't get any reaction from Ben or Roy when he told them he was going out with someone other than Mandy. Not so much as a raised eyebrow. Not even when he told them she was picking him up. He knew they'd discuss it after he left, which was a short time later.

The bar was as quiet as it was the first time they were there. There was only one young couple in a booth and a well-dressed older man at the bar. They were well into a pitcher of beer, and Mack had listened to a lot of Wanda's idle chatter before he remembered who the man at the bar was. They'd off and on studied each other, and he seemed to be as curious about Mack as Mack was about him. When the man at the bar realized who Mack was, he walked over to their booth, carrying the glass of beer he'd been nursing.

"Hello, Mack," he said, "mind if I join you?"

"Not a bit," Mack said, motioning for Harley Anderson, the former president of the Kingsburg State Bank, to sit down. "This is Wanda, Mr. Anderson."

Harley smiled at Wanda, nodded thanks, and sat down across from Mack, next to her. He raised his hand and flipped it at the bartender, who appeared quickly with a pitcher of beer.

"How's everything," Harley asked, "with you and your dad?"

"Things are lousy, as you probably know. We're okay otherwise."

"Yes…well, I can't say I approve of the way the bank is going about handling your dad's account, even if the bank is only a small part of the project. However, when it's completed, the project will be an economic benefit to the whole community."

"What is this project the bank's involved in?"

"I can't give you the details. I can only tell you that it's much bigger than you're likely to believe. The construction alone will bring millions into the local economy."

"What you really mean is that the rich around here are going to get richer."

"Nothing of the kind. Workers involved in any and all phases of construction will benefit via full employment. It might even be something for you to look into, Mack, now that you're back home. It pays a lot better than farming ever will."

"It's still working for wages. I'd rather farm and be my own man."

"That's not a very good attitude in this day and age. I'm not sure it ever was. Progress moves a lot faster when people work together with a common goal."

"The trouble is, Mr. Anderson, I don't very often agree with progress. Not the kind that's based only on money and profits, with no regard to anything else that matters."

"I assure you, Mack, this project is a lot more than money and profits. It will improve the economy of the entire area and the lives of nearly everyone who lives here. The benefits are enormous. The permanent full-time jobs it will provide will benefit a few hundred people."

"The costs to the environment are enormous too. If the real costs were ever considered, it would never happen."

"I understand how you feel, with your dad having to sell out. That's something I feel bad about and wish I could change. If he had sold the farm when the corporation made its offer, he wouldn't be in the trouble he's in. It's not the fault of the bank, the corporation, or this project that he's in the bind he's in. It's nature and the fact he's been so stubborn. Now, because of him, there've been cost overruns from the delays on the start of construction, so the corporation is no longer willing to match their original offer."

"I'm not at all sure, Mr. Anderson," Mack said, trying to curb his growing irritation with this man he grew up respecting as honest and fair, "I don't believe nature had anything to do with Dad's crop failures."

"What do you mean by that, Mack?"

"I mean that it doesn't look like disease or drought. The land is good, as it should be after all the work Dad's done to improve it. About the only thing I've ever seen do the kind of damage his crops appear to be suffering from is herbicides. Never to the scale done now, of course. When accidents happened in the past, the damage was relatively minor and only around the edges of the fields. Not his whole crop."

"You don't really believe someone intentionally destroyed his crops?"

"I don't know. All I know is that it looks like herbicide damage. There's no way of knowing for sure, one way or the other."

"Have the soil tested for pesticide residue, Mack. It's something you should find out, and I'd really like to know. There's certainly no excuse for it, if that's what it is."

"Who can I get to test the soil? And what will it cost?"

"The county agent can do it for you, I should think. It's not expensive. If he can't do it, he'll know who can."

"I'll mention it to Dad."

"Good. Let me know what the results are. As much as I believe in the project, it'd bother me a great deal if anyone involved did something so wrong and so stupid, as destroying your dad's crops."

"I'm curious about something, Mr. Anderson. Why didn't anyone explain to Dad why the bank wanted his land? Why the big secret about the project?"

"Until recently, there've been some very delicate negotiations going on with the folks in Washington. The deal was nearly made a few years ago. Then the Republicans lost the presidency, and it hit quite a few snags. It couldn't be completed until the Republicans had their last big wins. Thank God they did."

"I don't think I'd blame any god for it. Looks more like the devil's work to me."

"Really? You surprise me. Most farmers, and most cowboys for that matter, tend to be rather conservative."

"So do I, in a real sense, though, not a political one. The environment has been damaged by them, far more than it should've been. In recent years, it's been a disaster."

"That's not only the conservative's doing, it's all of us. But I think I should be going now. My wife will be worrying if I'm not home soon. I never have more than one or two beers, and thanks to you, I've had three." He stood to leave. "You take care, Mack. You too, young lady. I enjoyed our conversation very much."

Mack and Wanda watched him leave before either of them said anything.

"You kind of surprise me, Mack," she said. "Talking a deputy sheriff out of arresting me took a lot, even if we did go to school with him. Being able to sit down and talk with a bank president like he's your old buddy, that takes a lot more."

"Not really. Most of the time, if you treat people like they're ordinary folks, they act like it."

"Boy, you've sure grown up to be something. Not just a gentleman, you're a cowboy philosopher too."

"I'm neither. I'm pretty ordinary."

"No, Mack, you're not quite what I'd call ordinary. Now tell me what this big project is about. I've never heard about it before."

Mack told her what he knew.

"Wow, you mean they're going to use part of the refuge? That's something I never thought would happen. I'm not sure I agree with you about it, though. Aren't people more important than having a place for trees and a bunch of animals?"

"Sure, people are important. That's not what this is about. Unless you think about people on a long-term basis. Long term, the project is going to turn out to be the worst thing that could happen to this area."

"I think you're wrong. People are what it's about. Having decent jobs is important. So's progress. Improving the economy around here is real progress as far as I'm concerned, and it's what we need."

"All it's going to do is make it as crowded here as it is in any suburb. If you want that, why not move closer to the cities?"

"This is where I live. Why should I have to move to get a better job?"

"It depends on what you mean by a better job."

"One that pays better."

"All I can say is, wait and see."

"Okay, Mack, only let's not argue about it anymore."

"Okay."

"Once again, a gentleman."

"No, I don't think so."

"Yes, you are. I want to change the subject and you do it for me. The other night, though, what you did was really special."

"What did I do? Other than let you drive away from here when I knew you drank too much. I wasn't being a gentleman. I was so tied up in myself that I didn't pay enough attention to you and do what I should have."

She laughed. "That's nonsense and we both know it."

Wanda went to the bar and bought another pitcher of beer. After bringing it to the booth, she went to the jukebox and dropped some coins in. She took his hand and pulled him out of the booth. Mack thought they fit together okay as they danced to five slow country songs.

They finished their beer, then left the bar. She drove as many little-used country roads as she could, driving several extra miles. Their talk was idle chatter, interspersed with quiet. Mack stayed on his side of the car.

"Mack," she said, as they got closer to the farm, "you're not going to try anything with me tonight, are you?"

"Nope."

"I was afraid of that. Mind if I ask why? I know I'm not real pretty, but I'm not ugly either."

"You're plenty good looking, Wanda. Looks don't have anything to do with it."

"What is it then? Do you just not like me, is it because I talk too much, or what?

"Nothing like that. I've got some things happening in my life right now. I've got to figure them out before I can get involved with anyone."

"After you do?"

"I don't know. Let's wait and see."

"Tell me when you know. I know I'm being forward, but I have this feeling I don't have enough time to wait around and do things the way a nice, proper girl ought to. I think if I do, I'll lose."

"I'll let you know when I have things figured out, if there's something to tell you."

"Okay, I'll settle for that. And if there's ever anything I can do for you, tell me that too."

"Sure. You can go out with me again tomorrow night." Wanda smiled.

"Nothing I'd rather do. What time?"

"About eight."

"Do you have anything special in mind?" Her smile broadened.

"Well, I'm kind of short on cash, so how about going for a walk?"

"Where?" Her smile slipped.

"There's a couple of nice trails in the refuge."

She glared at him for a minute, then smiled again. "Okay, I'll pick you up."

Chapter 17

Sleeping was difficult for Mack after Wanda dropped him off. He couldn't shake his worry about Mandy, his concern for Ben and the farm he was losing, or his anger at those who were about to destroy the refuge he loved. It was well into the early morning hours before his mind let go enough for him to sleep. Even then, it was filled with bad dreams.

His head was still spinning when he woke up with the sun in his eyes. Knowing instantly he'd slept too late, he jumped upright in bed, sending an all too familiar pain searing through his back, slowing him down and frustrating him even further.

Ben and Roy had long since left the house, so he went out to find them without bothering with breakfast or even coffee. They were working on an old plow in the machine shed, which Ben hadn't used since before Mack left home to ride bulls.

"Why," Mack asked, "are you working on that piece of junk?"

Roy grinned. "A little fixing, along with a new coat of paint, and this fine plow ought to bring a good price at the auction. Other than the lack of hydraulics, there's nothing wrong with it. Ben did plenty of plowing with it."

"The only reason I stopped using it," Ben said, "was because I got a better plow."

"I talked to Harley Anderson last night. Ran across him at a bar. There definitely is some kind of project in the works. It'll probably be a big resort, and it'll be connected with the refuge. Some big corporation is involved in it, along with the bank."

"That does explain," Ben said, "the bank leaning so hard on me for the money. There still isn't anything we can do about it."

"He also said we can have the soil tested for pesticide residue. If we find any, then we'll know what's been killing the crops."

"You think someone sprayed my crops to kill them?"

"I do. We both know who's behind it. Harley told me you've been costing the project money. Your not selling the farm to them has held up the start of construction."

"How do I get the soil tested?"

"Harley said to call the county agent. If he can't get it done, he should know who can."

"I'm sure now that you're right, Mack. The crops look like they've been sprayed, and now we know why. Someone could've done it on weekends when I was at the farmer's market. If they sprayed early in the day, from the air, I wouldn't have noticed it when I got home."

"Neither would the neighbors since there aren't any left."

Mack went back in the house and called Mandy at work, hoping she could find a way to see him that night.

"I'm sorry, Mack," she said, speaking carefully, "I can't see you. I won't be able to see you again until after the auction."

"Why not? What's going on? Or is all we said to each other yesterday only a lot of meaningless words?"

"I meant every word, Mack. I do love you. You'll just have to be patient. Please trust me."

"There's something wrong that you're not telling me."

"It's not serious, and it's nothing you can help me with."

"How can I know that if you won't tell what me it is?"

"What makes you so sure there's anything you can do?"

"I'm not. Not until I know what's wrong."

"I'm sorry, Mack, I've really got to go. I'll get into trouble if I talk too long."

She hung up.

There was still a lot of day left to work, so Mack went out and started patching a side of the barn. He didn't get far before Ben and Roy joined him.

"There something troubling you, Mack?" Ben asked.

"Only every damn thing I can think of."

"Maybe you'd best go do something then, about every damn thing, before you up and kill this poor barn with your hammer. I know it's older than me even, but I don't think it's ready for its grave yet."

"You're right. Mind if I borrow your truck, Roy?"

"Only if you promise me you won't treat it the way you been fixing this here barn." He laughed.

Mack went inside the house and took a long cold shower, more to kill frustration than to beat the heat, which was building again.

It would be hours before Mandy got off work, so he couldn't drive down to see her right away. He called Dale Magee instead, at the number on the back of the card he'd given Mack.

"What's up, Mack?" Dale asked when he answered the phone.

"I was wondering if you had time for a beer this afternoon?"

"I've got time. I better stick to coffee though. I'm working tonight. Let's meet at Katie's in about an hour."

"Sounds good."

Mack sat down in the first empty booth he saw when he arrived early at Katie's Kafe on the main street of Kingsburg. Before he was waited on, someone tapped him lightly on his shoulder.

"Too good to have me wait on you?" Wanda asked, moving to his side and putting her hands on her hips.

"No," he smiled. "Wait on me."

"I can't. You're in the wrong section."

"I didn't know that. I didn't even know you worked here."

She returned his smile. "No, I guess you didn't. Move over to the other side."

She pointed to the area she wanted him to sit. He moved.

"What can I get you?" she asked when he was settled.

"Coffee for now. I'll wait until Dale gets here before I decide whether to have anything else."

"Until who gets here?"

"Dale Magee. You remember him from the other night, don't you?"

"I remember him, yes." She blushed. "The other night, no."

She quickly brought him his coffee. “I think I’d have been better off leaving you over there,” she said, then disappeared.

Mack was on his second cup when Dale joined him.

“So how’s it going with you?” Dale asked.

“Okay, I guess.”

“You don’t sound very enthusiastic, Mack. To tell you the truth, I was kind of hoping you’d called me on a social basis. You know, like two old high school pals, which I know we weren’t. What’s on your mind?”

“A few things, but if I’m taking advantage, let’s just have coffee, talk some, and let it go at that.”

“Sorry, Mack. I guess I’m getting a little too defensive about the job. Sometimes, people want the damnedest things from me.”

“It’s okay, Dale. I understand how it can go. And I do owe you an apology. I was taking advantage. Let’s let it go. I doubt you can do anything about what’s on my mind anyway. Why don’t you tell me what, besides being a cop, you’ve done with yourself since we graduated from the wonderful institution of high school?”

“You make it sound as though we were in jail.”

“It often felt like it.”

Wanda walked up to the booth.

“Hi, Dale,” she said, her voice hesitant and her face a deep crimson, “what can I get for you?”

“Wanda, hi,” he answered, his face breaking into a pleasant smile. “You’re looking good today. Been getting some sun?”

“No,” she answered, coloring deeper.

Mack laughed. “It’s okay, Wanda. All we’re doing is having a bit of a high school reunion today.”

Wanda’s eyes shot him daggers. “What can I get you, Dale?”

“Coffee will do it for now.”

She nodded and went for his coffee.

“I take it,” Dale said, “she’s embarrassed about the other night.”

“She is. All the more so because it isn’t something she makes a habit of. She isn’t used to drinking, so before she realized, she was out of control and in trouble.”

“Yeah, I understand. I’ve done it a time or two myself.”

"Me too."

"Since we have that settled, tell me why you called and wanted to see me today."

"Just some things that, as I said, you probably can't give me any answers for."

"I don't think you're the type of person who'd be asking trivial questions. Now you've got my curiosity going, so I'd prefer you ask away."

"Okay. To start with, what do you know about the project that's going to be built in part of the refuge?"

"Not much. Only that it's big and will bring a lot of money into this area. Should be a real boost to the economy around here."

"You bet it will," Mack answered, his voice filled with sarcasm.

"What's your problem with it, Mack?" Dale asked, a bewildered look on his face.

"Hundreds of things. On a personal basis, my dad's losing his farm because of it."

"They're buying it from him, aren't they?"

"No, it's going up for auction in a couple of weeks. Only because someone poisoned his crops the past two years. He's broke now and has no choice except to sell out."

"What do you mean, someone's poisoned his crops? How could they?"

"Herbicides. Most common herbicides kill vegetable crops. Someone sprayed them to force him to sell out."

"Can you prove it?"

"Not until the soil's tested. When it is, we'll have proof it was done. It's pretty obvious to me who's behind it, but I don't see how we'll ever find a way to prove it."

"How was it done?"

"Has to have been from the air. On Saturdays, when Dad was at the Minneapolis farmer's market. It's the only time he's away from home on a regular basis. He goes on Sundays too, but not always. He doesn't always have enough vegetables left after Saturday's sales to make it worth the trip."

"You think they were sprayed more than once?"

"No doubt about it. If it was done all at the same time, it would've been way too obvious. The only things that take all the crops at once are wind or hail. Not even drought will kill them all at the same time. Insects tend to be specific to one or two crops. Besides, there's no sign of any bug problem. We haven't had any really bad winds or hail the last two years. Even if we had, Dad's been hit with both at one time or another and gotten a crop anyway."

"How did he manage that?"

"He's an organic farmer. His ground is rich and healthy. If it wasn't, he probably would've lost his crops when we had bad weather. He also does a lot of work by hand, and sometimes, he simply replanted the damaged crops. With the same crop when he could, something else when he couldn't. There's a lot of vegetable crops that can be planted as late as August. Nothing worked for him the last two years. What he replanted died or didn't come up at all. The only thing that hasn't died is the sweet corn. Herbicides used on corn will kill all the other vegetables he raises."

"Maybe he used too much spray on his corn."

"No. Like I said, he's an organic farmer. That means he never uses pesticides of any kind. He doesn't even use commercial fertilizers. Everything is done as naturally as possible."

"I thought all the ground over there was blow sand. That's part of the reason why they managed to turn it into a refuge in the first place. It wasn't worth much for farming. So how could he ever expect to get a crop?"

"When Dad bought the place, it wasn't good ground. When you follow the right farming practices, sand makes a real nice medium for growing vegetables. Almost anything else as far as that goes. It wasn't easy, but his ground improved every year. Stop by sometime and I'll show you."

"I will. I'd like to see it. It sounds interesting. Now, about not being able to prove who sprayed your dad's crops, first get me proof that they were in fact sprayed, then let me see if I can find out who did it."

"How are you going to do that?"

"The someone who did the actual spraying has to own the equipment. It isn't cheap, especially not if it's done from the air. The odds are it was a professional. There aren't many around who do the work."

"That makes sense."

"Didn't you have some more questions, Mack?"

"This is enough for now. The rest are real personal. I think, after this conversation, I'll find some more answers before I dump any questions about them on you."

"You sure?"

"I am."

"I have one for you then."

"Shoot."

"Well, ah," Dale hesitated, "are you and Wanda dating?"

"No, not really. We're mostly just friends. We go out, but it's nothing serious. Like the date we've got tonight. We're going over to the refuge and walk one of the trails."

"Which one? I'm only curious because I've done some hiking over there myself."

"Probably the schoolhouse trail. It's the easiest walking. I'm not sure how used to hiking Wanda is."

"It sounds like fun. Now, I better get rolling. I've got a few things to do before I get ready for work."

"Thanks for your time, Dale. I do appreciate it."

"Anytime. Let's for sure have a beer some night."

"You bet."

Dale reached in his pocket as he stood to leave. Mack waved him off.

"I'll take care of it, Dale," he said.

"I'll get it next time then," Dale said. He waved a hand and left. Wanda returned to the booth almost immediately.

"I think I should be mad at you," she grumbled, "embarrassing me like that."

"Do you still want to go out tonight?"

"Sure," she smiled. "Maybe after today, I'll get you to do more than talk. You owe me one now."

"We'll see," Mack said, dropping a couple of dollars on the table and leaving the cafe.

Chapter 18

Dale Magee sat down at the bar and ordered a Pepsi. He was still in civilian clothes, wearing jeans, plaid shirt, and a baseball cap with an extra-large brim, pulled down low on his forehead. His back was to the tables and booths. He watched them in the mirror behind the bar.

They came in one at a time. The big man was sitting in the booth when Dale went in. The suit he was wearing was obviously too small, and his huge gut stuck out, hanging over his belt. Even though he was out of uniform, Dale knew the sheriff from his figure alone, without seeing his face.

After leaving Katie's Kafe, Dale followed him to the bar, located ten minutes out of the county. The woman arrived shortly after the sheriff, still in her refuge uniform. Jason was ten minutes behind the first two and came in acting agitated and in a hurry.

The three of them sat in a booth too far from Dale for him to pick up any more than snatches of their conversation. What he did hear was enough to tell him they were disagreeing about something they were planning. What interested him the most were the words *dead* and *accident*, then something about Mack Thomas.

It was enough to convince Dale that what Mack told him at Katie's Kafe was probably true. Apparently, these three were involved in more than he already suspected. He was equally sure now that the many times he'd watched them since the death of Ray Foss were worthwhile.

Fifteen minutes later, Dale realized the Pepsi, along with the coffee he drank earlier, was having a strong effect on him, even though he was only on his second Pepsi. He needed to use the restroom, but to get to it, he needed to walk by their booth. It was a long, uncomfortable ten minutes before the sheriff abruptly left, his manner indicating he was angry. Dale waited another five minutes, then could wait no longer. He kept his head down as he hurried to the restroom, hoping Jason wouldn't notice him. The woman kept her eyes completely focused on Jason. He was talking as Dale walked past the booth.

"Listen, Elaine," Jason said, "I'd like to stay and have another drink with you. I can't if I'm going to meet you at our spot tonight. There are some things I've got to finish up at the bank first. Either I stay now or go tonight. I can't do both."

"Yes sure, leave, after I went ahead and let the jerk get all upset with me." She turned her head and stared at the wall. "I'll see you tonight. You better be on time. I won't be waiting around for you. You don't want to have to settle for your wife, do you?"

"Now, Elaine," Jason answered, laying what he considered to be his most charming smile on her, "don't be that way."

Good old Jason, Dale thought, *he's still at it.* One would have thought he'd have run out of women by now or that women would have learned to see through him.

Jason was not one of his favorite people, and now Dale had another reason to watch him. The spot Jason referred to might hold some answers, however small they proved to be.

Tonight, Dale decided, might be a good time to find out where that special place of theirs was.

Chapter 19

Mack hadn't driven to the Twin Cities for years, so he left directly from Kingsburg to give himself extra time to get there and find Mandy's office building. He got lost twice looking for it and still had over an hour to wait when he finally found it.

The time wasn't wasted. There was no place to park near the entrance of the building, and instead of one huge parking lot, parking was divided up into several small lots on different levels, built to match the natural grade of the land. Mack had no idea where Mandy was parked, and with trees and shrubs filling the spaces between the parking areas, he was forced to drive through each of them as he searched for her car. He was sure he'd missed it until he finally found her car in a small section, near the entrance to the office building, that he hadn't noticed when he first got there.

People were already leaving work by then, and it was only a short time later that Mandy came out of the building and walked to her car. She stopped as soon as she saw Mack, turned around, and hurried back inside the building. He was determined to talk to her, so he left the truck where it was and went inside after her.

As soon as she saw him coming, she knew it wouldn't do any good to run and let him take her hand and lead her back outside. She didn't say a word until they were inside the truck and he took off the dark glasses she was wearing.

"Another cabinet door?" he asked, pointing at her black eye.

"It's nothing, Mack," she said, trying to smile, but not quite managing it. "So don't worry about it."

"Why did the son of a bitch do it this time?"

"It doesn't really matter, and I certainly don't need you doing something stupid right now."

"How am I supposed to ignore this? I ought to kill Jason."

"Please, don't..." Mandy started crying.

Mack hated watching her cry, so he held her until she stopped, then kissed her.

"You have to promise me, Mack," she said as she calmed down, "you won't do anything. I'm okay and I am going to leave him. I just need more time."

"For what? More beatings?"

"Please, Mack, don't let your temper do your thinking. I've got some things to do before I can leave him. You've got to trust me on this. I want you to promise me you won't do anything to Jason. Fighting with him is no solution."

"I can't. I'll give you time because you say you need it. I will not promise he's going to walk away without me paying him a visit. Especially not if this kind of crap continues."

"Time then. Give me time."

"Okay."

"Thank you. I wish I could stay with you now, I just can't. I've got to get home."

"Why, so he won't beat you up again?"

"Mack, you promised..."

"I know, I know. It isn't easy to let you go back to that coward. What he's doing for the bank isn't enough, he's got to be hurting you too. Just about the lowest form of life there is are men who beat women."

"That's one of the things I need time for. Why is he doing what he's doing? I don't think it's only for the bank."

"Do you have some ideas?"

"Nothing worth talking about yet. Give me the time I need and maybe I will."

"How?"

"His computer. He doesn't know I've learned how to use one at work. I still have a lot to learn about the miserable things. I think I might know enough now to check into what he's doing and what his real connection with the project is."

"You think he keeps records at home?"

"I know he does. I don't know what, exactly, they're going to tell me. Or even if I can get access to them. I'm still going to try. Now I have to go." She kissed him hard. "Remember, I love you. I'll call you when I can."

Mack felt his stomach tighten as he watched her walk away. It stayed tight all the way back to the farm. He couldn't eat supper when he got there.

"It isn't like you to skip eating, Mack," Ben said, his concern showing. "I take it you didn't solve much today."

"Not too much. Jason's been beating her again."

"What are you planning to do about it?"

"Nothing yet. She asked for more time before she leaves him. I promised to give her some."

"You aren't thinking of doing something stupid, are you?"

"Like what?"

"Like hunting up Jason."

"Not yet."

"Don't do it. He isn't worth it. No point to it anyhow. You can't whip him with your back screwed up the way it is."

"It doesn't matter. Either way, he will know he's been in a fight. He, for sure, will know what pain is when it's done."

"I don't doubt you can hurt him. Do what Mandy asked anyway. You do, and likely as not, the two of you can walk away without any trouble. You'll hurt him in a way you can't get to him with a beating. You'll hurt his pride."

"You're right. I still hate walking away from a man who beats a woman. It seems to me, he ought to get some of what he gives."

"I can't say he shouldn't. Thing is, you ought to know that he isn't a real man. He isn't ever going to have anything worth having, no matter how much money he manages to grab on to. Sooner or later, he'll get his due."

"If he does, it'd be a pure pleasure to be the one who gives it to him. It's hard for me to believe that I ever called him a friend."

"People change, Mack. Maybe there are reasons why he grew up the way he did."

"I still don't see any excuse."

"No, there aren't any excuses. What he's let himself become makes him just so much shit you don't want to be stepping in."

"Be nice if we could prove he's the one who had your crops sprayed."

"The county agent was out today. He took a lot of soil samples to test."

"When will we know the results?"

"A couple of days. No more than a week."

"Be nice if it was before the auction."

"I don't think we can stop it, anyway, Mack, no matter what he finds."

"Maybe not, but I'd sure like the chance to try."

Chapter 20

After Mack finished talking to Ben and Roy, he tried to relax. He paced the floor, went outside, and walked around the yard, through the buildings, and around the yard again. The tension he felt only got worse, so he went back inside the house and called Wanda, asking her to come over earlier than they'd planned. He felt as though he needed to do something, anything, right away, or he'd explode.

She picked him up again, drove straight to the refuge, and parked in the old schoolhouse lot. She surprised him when she reached into the back seat, opened a large cooler, and took out two cans of beer.

"I brought the bar with us tonight. Thought you might enjoy a few beers when it's so hot."

"Great," Mack said, opening the can and pouring half of it down.

"We'd cool off," Wanda said, smiling, "if we undressed."

"Now, Wanda, behave yourself."

"Sure. Is it okay if I take my bra off? I shouldn't have worn this one. It's itching like crazy."

Mack laughed. "Take it off. It doesn't look like we'll be doing much walking."

"Probably not. It's too hot. You don't have to watch me do this if it bothers you."

"It's a nice way to get bothered."

Wanda knew what she was doing as she slowly opened her blouse and slid it off her shoulders. She threw her shoulders back as she reached behind her to unhook her bra, making her ample breasts seem even larger. The blouse went on as slow as it came off, and she gave up on the buttons after the bottom three. Her nipples protruded gently against the soft material of the blouse.

Mack finished his beer in one gulp, then took out another and opened it.

"Don't I do anything for you, Mack?" she asked, pushing her lips into a mock pout.

"You do a lot. You're not the problem. Life is."

"Like how? Have you already got a girl?"

"I think so. I'm not sure yet."

"What does that mean? You're talking in circles."

"It was only a couple of days ago when someone gave me hell for being too direct. Now you tell me I'm talking in circles. I'm confused."

"Apparently. You didn't answer my question."

"She's married."

"Wonderful! I'm hung up on you, you're hung up on her, and I suppose she's hung up on her husband. What a screwed-up world. How did I get myself into this?"

"The same way I did, I guess. You expect life to move in a straight line, and instead, it keeps knocking you off in a different direction."

"There you go again, Mack, being a damn philosopher." Wanda laughed, then asked, "Who is she? Or is my asking prying too much?"

He told her all about Mandy.

"I know Mandy, by the way. Her husband Jason is a real jerk. In high school, he was always touching, then trying to pretend it was an accident."

"From what I remember, he pretty much got away with it. Most of the girls liked Jason."

"Not me! He asked me out once."

"Did you have a good time?"

"I didn't go. All he wanted was the chance to get his hands all over what you're trying so hard to ignore."

"It does take a lot of effort."

"Good. So what are you going to do, Mack?"

"Wait, like she asked me to."

"Do you expect me to wait too?"

"No."

"Do you want me to?"

"It wouldn't be fair if I did, would it?"

"What is? I've mostly made a mess out of my life so far. Always picking the wrong guy. I even married one of them once. Only lasted a year. It seems like nothing ever lasts. I think I'll wait around for a while. You might be worth waiting for."

"I'd hate to see you hurt, Wanda. I really like you."

"Well, that's a start. I like you too. You're more honest and kind than most men I've known. There's a gentle streak running under your pretend tough exterior. I can't see you ever being mean or abusive."

"You think you have me all figured out, don't you."

"Quite the contrary. I seriously doubt I'll ever totally understand you. And that makes you more interesting."

"It does?"

"Yes, it most certainly does."

"What the hell is it about me you don't understand?"

"How you can be yourself and the way you seem to want to do what's right, even if it costs you. Most people aren't always willing to do what's right if it costs them."

"I think what a person does depends more on how life strikes them than on what happens."

Wanda laughed again. "You definitely are a philosopher. A cowboy philosopher."

"Like Will Rogers, huh?"

"Not nowhere near that good. If you keep this up though, I'm going to fall in love with you."

"Don't. It would be a mistake. A big one."

"Why?"

"You can do better than a broken-down cowboy who doesn't know where he's headed in life."

"You're a lot more than a broken-down cowboy, Mack. You're a good man who's at a crossroads in life. You just haven't figured out which road to take yet."

"Maybe. I've never made any money. I'm broke now. I can't say there'd ever be more than a friendship between us. You deserve more."

"I think I'll hang around long enough to be sure of that. Will you do something for me now?"

"Sure, what?"

"Hold me. Please, just hold me."

Chapter 21

Not long after Dale Magee started work, he drove to Kingsburg's City Hall, next to the bank on main street. He had some papers to deliver for the sheriff, as he often did, so no one paid any attention when he parked and went inside. While he watched the bank parking lot, he stalled for time by flirting with the pretty young clerk at the reception desk. The ploy worked until Jason came out of the bank. Dale stammered an apology as he rushed out, leaving the young lady wondering what he was up to. She'd been hoping for a long time that he'd ask her out, and this time, it seemed as if he was about to. It disappointed her when he didn't. It would have disappointed Dale even more if he'd known that. Dale reached his squad car as Jason sped out onto the street, kicking up some loose gravel and squealing his tires.

"I ought to pull him over," Dale mumbled to himself as he followed Jason. "I'd enjoy giving him a ticket."

He was forced to stay well behind Jason while he followed. The police car he was driving was too conspicuous to allow him to follow close. He stayed with Jason as he traveled south out of town, then west, and south again along the south leg of the refuge. He lost him after a series of curves in the county road. Since there were too many roads Jason might have taken and places he could have gone, Dale knew it was pointless to search for him. Instead, he decided to cruise around for a while, on the chance he would run across him again.

When he got to the far end of the refuge, from the spot he lost Jason, he remembered what Mack told him about his date with Wanda and drove to the old schoolhouse to see if they were still around. He pulled into the parking lot and stopped next to her car when he found them there.

"If I felt like being a jerk tonight," he said, getting out of his car, "I could hang you guys for drinking beer here."

"We aren't drinking, Dale," Wanda explained, "we're parked and only having a beer. Oh, by the way, thanks for the other night. I should have told you that earlier today."

"You're welcome, Wanda," Dale said, smiling. "Just don't spread it around. So tell me, while you've been parked and only drinking one beer, did you see any other cars driving around?"

"Not a one," Mack answered, getting out of the car. "Are you looking for someone?"

"Yeah."

"Do you mind telling me who?"

"Well, ah…"

"I take it you'd rather not say."

Dale shrugged.

"It must be someone I know then. If it is, I'd guess it's Jason Cheman. Is it?"

"I'm not sure I should tell you, Mack."

"What did he do, poke the wrong lady this time?"

"Not this time," Dale answered, a surprised smile on his face, "unless he gets caught by the husband. I find it interesting, though, that you're reacting this way. I thought you were a friend of his."

"I was, once. Considering all that's going on around here, most of which Jason is, I think, involved in, I really don't believe I can call him a friend. Why're you looking for him?"

"I'm not, exactly. I happen to know he's around here somewhere, and I'm curious why. I think there's more to it than the lady he's meeting."

"Who is she?"

"Does it matter?"

"I don't know for sure. It could. I know for sure he's got one, maybe two on the side. One works for the refuge. Her name's Elaine."

"How did you know?"

"This is kind of embarrassing. The other night when I was out for a walk in the refuge…" Mack explained to Dale what he saw happen between Jason and Elaine.

"What he did couldn't have bothered her a hell of a lot. He's meeting her around here tonight. I was tailing him. Lost him on the west side of the south leg too."

"Why were you following him?"

"I'd rather not say."

"Why not? Even if it's official police business, you know that if there's a chance it has a connection to what's happening to my dad, it's important to me."

"Actually, it's not official. It's more of a personal curiosity about something."

"Has it got anything to do with what we talked about this morning?"

"I'm not sure. Remember Ray Foss? He used to manage this refuge."

"Yes. I heard he killed himself."

"I was the first deputy there when the call came in about the shooting."

"You think he committed suicide?"

"I'm not sure."

"Personally, I don't understand why he would. I knew Ray a long time. He was one of the few people I ever knew who really loved what he did. He also believed his work meant something. I rode bulls because I wanted to, and that was reason enough for me. What Ray did was good for everyone. For the whole planet as far as that goes. I met his family. He really cared about them. So I can't think of a reason he'd do it."

"I don't have any answers, Mack. That's why I was following Jason and why I've been watching him for nearly a year now."

"Maybe Ray was murdered for some reason connected with this wonderful project? Maybe he was killed for being against selling part of the refuge to create a playland for the rich. I doubt even the fools in Washington could get away with doing it without some support from the refuge staff. They'd have to go along to keep the locals from knowing the real impact the resort is going to have on the refuge. The damage is going to be far more than the loss of the south leg."

"I guess that's possible," Dale answered.

"You mean you do think he was murdered?"

"Again, I'm not positive. I was there right after it happened, and it plain didn't feel right."

"How?"

"It was little things that bothered me. A bare spot...a round bare spot on a shelf in his office, with a light layer of dust all around it. A piece of glass on the floor close by, like something was broken and then cleaned up. He died with his chair pushed way back from his desk. Blew out the back of his head, all over the records on the shelves behind him. Made an awful a mess. From the looks of the rest of his office, he was one of those people who was meticulously organized, yet those records were dumped on the shelves every which way. I guess the only reason I noticed them was because of the mess the back of his head made. The sheriff said I was inexperienced and shouldn't try to play detective. It was a suicide and I was to mind my manners and tend to business. Then he had me call the coroner to get the body. There was no autopsy done. I've been watching the sheriff ever since, which has led me to watching Jason and the refuge woman."

"I thought the coroner always did an autopsy when it's a violent death?"

"Not in this county, Mack. When we want a death checked out properly, we call a medical examiner. In this county, the coroner is elected. He doesn't know anything about forensic medicine."

"What has all this got to do with following Jason tonight?"

"There's too many times that I've seen him, Jason, and this Elaine getting together in quiet, out-of-town places. Like they're having some kind of meeting. Also, in the past, the sheriff was always hell on drug dealers. He still is, except for a couple of locals. With those two, it's been mostly hands off. Jason's a banker. Sometimes, money needs hiding and cleaning..."

"No kidding? Nothing Jason does can surprise me. And he does have something going with the woman."

"It's funny. Most of the time, they don't act as though they like each other much. When I see the three of them together, she's been a lot friendlier with the sheriff than she is with Jason. Until recently, she'd leave those meetings with the sheriff, not Jason. Usually, they spent some time in her van."

"Who is Elaine? Where'd she come from? She wasn't at the refuge a few years ago."

"I don't know anything about her. She was the one who put in the call on Ray. She found his body. Said she was there to pick up her husband. He was working that Saturday. Doing some kind of study out in the field. The thing is, he didn't get to the office until after we did. Why was she there so early? And why the hell was Ray there that day?"

"It probably wasn't unusual for Ray to work on a Saturday. He was pretty dedicated. What's all this about her husband?"

"He works at the refuge. If I remember it right, they weren't married very long at the time."

"Which one of the guys is it, Dale?"

"I think it was Rick, Rich, something like that."

"I know Rich pretty well. He's already married. He was a few years ago anyway."

"It could be someone else. I can check it out and let you know."

"I'd appreciate it. He's a good man. I'd sure hate to see him get screwed around by her this way. I'll have to watch what I say next time I talk to him."

"You've been talking to him?"

"Once. I stopped by the refuge to say hello."

"That the only reason?"

"No. I was also trying to find out about the project. I talked to him and Jerry Mason, the refuge biologist. Neither one had a lot to say. They're trying to keep a low profile on what's going on."

"I think you ought to be careful, Mack."

"Why?"

"You might be getting the wrong people worried."

"I doubt it. What could I do that would bother anyone? I'm just a dumb cowboy."

"Sure. Watch your backside anyway."

"You have another reason why you're so concerned all the sudden? You didn't seem to be this morning."

"Late this afternoon, I was in the same bar as Jason and company, trying to listen in on one of their little meetings. I didn't hear much, only snatches. Three words were *dead*, *accident*, and *Mack Thomas*. Not that far apart, either."

"There might be something to what you're saying." Mack went on to tell Dale about the shots fired into the side of the barn.

"Mack, if you aren't careful, there's no telling what's going to happen. From the way this is shaping up, I'd say there's more going on than either one of us suspected."

"I think you're right. I'll be more careful. As long as this is hurting my dad though, I'm not backing off entirely."

"I don't expect you to. Do you really think the refuge will be damaged when they build the project?"

"I know it will. Far more than most people will realize, even after they finish the project."

"The economy around here does need the boost."

"It won't be improved. What the project is actually going to do is bring in more people, crime, the need for more schools and roads and services. Wait and see. The place where we grew up is on its way down the toilet."

"I never thought of it that way."

"Nobody else has either."

Chapter 22

It was late when Wanda brought Mack home, so he woke up tired. Until Ben told him, he didn't realize that it was Friday, the day Ben always spent washing and sorting his vegetables to prepare them for the farmer's market.

While Ben worked on them, Mack helped Roy haul old machinery out of a patch of woods near the barn. Some of it was abandoned long before Ben bought the place and the rest were machines Ben wore out or replaced, then dumped there.

"You know, Mack," Roy said, "some of this stuff is really old. Near a hundred years. If we get some collectors at this auction, it'll bring a decent price if we clean it up. This other stuff that was Ben's, we can fix it some so it works again, give it a coat of paint, and the hobby farmers who come might be willing to buy it. Even if it does take some time, I think it'll prove to be worth it."

"Could be," Mack agreed. "Let's do it."

For the rest of the day, Mack worked on the oldest machinery, pulling out weeds tangled in wheels, gears, and levers, and cleaning it enough to be presentable. No attempts at repairs were made and nothing was painted. Anyone interested in machinery so old would likely be a collector and would want to do their own restoration.

Roy worked on the not quite so old machinery, repairing what he could, then painting it when it was in working order. The rest was left as it was, to be sold for scrap metal or parts. By the end of the day, when they quit to help Ben load the washed and sorted vegetables onto the trucks, Mack was beginning to think the auction might bring in more than enough to pay Ben's bills. Both trucks were overloaded by the time they finished loading all the vegetables. Ben was pleased to have salvaged so much, considering the disastrous state the crops were in.

"Should bring me enough cash to get by until the auction," he said. "Going to be a hell of a lot of work tomorrow, selling this much. You want to come along, Mack, and give us a hand?"

"You bet," Mack agreed. "It's been a long time since I've gone to the market. It might even be fun."

Mack found himself looking forward to going. It was a pleasant change from the almost constant feelings of concern he'd carried since he got off the early morning bus that brought him home. He went to bed before nine to be ready to enjoy a very early market.

A gentle touch of his shoulder and "It's time, Mack" from Ben left him feeling as if he'd barely closed his eyes. He groaned getting out of bed, continued to groan while he dressed, and groaned again when he staggered into the kitchen and looked at the clock. Three in the morning and nothing except dark outside the windows.

Ben pointed at a plate on the table, filled with a huge piece of fried steak, topped with four eggs.

"We don't have much time," Ben said, wiping his plate clean with a biscuit from a bowl in the center of the table, "so don't dwell on it. Just eat."

"There's a lot here to eat," Mack answered, with an already full mouth.

"You'll do her," Roy laughed, wiping his plate as Ben did.

After the first bite, Mack knew Roy was right. The steak was as tender as rare hamburger and went down as easily as ice cream on a hot day. He was finished before Ben and Roy drank their after breakfast mug of coffee.

"We've got a thermos of coffee going with us, Mack," Ben said as Mack wiped his plate clean, "and you can take your mug along. We'd best haul ass."

Mack shook his head, groaning as he stood up.

"And don't be groaning," Ben said, "it wasn't you who was woke up by the phone last night."

"You were?"

"Yeah, and both calls were for you."

"Who called?"

"Females, naturally. Who else would call at that late an hour on a market night? Wanda was about eleven. Mandy after midnight. Now get yourself into a truck. We're going."

Mack rode with Roy, running behind Ben. Roy still hadn't said much, so Mack kept quiet and tried to sleep. As soon as they got to the market, they started unloading.

Ben set up tables across the width of two stalls that he rented on an annual basis, then began filling small trays and baskets, his impatience with Mack and Roy obvious. The market was Ben's element, and other than work instructions from him, conversation was not tolerated. When Mack made a mistake, Ben cursed; when Roy did, he simply pointed it out. The display was filled and ready about an hour before the bulk of the customers began arriving, so Mack took the time to look around.

"Now don't be wasting too much time," Ben said as he left.

The market was filled with vendors. More than half were vegetable and fruit growers. In addition, there were fish, cheese, and produce dealers, florists, bakeries, people who raised, processed, and sold their own meat, and an odd assortment of artists, craft people, and even someone selling hand-built, wood patio furniture.

Mack stopped at a small cafe at the end of a long row of vendors to refill his coffee, then at a vendor who sold rich pastries. One corner stall was filled with houseplants, and down and across the aisle was a stall filled with honey.

He walked by truckloads of melons and sweet corn and huge piles of crated peaches and pears. In half of a stall, a young man sold wild rice in the other half, an older man was selling maple syrup. Samples of fruit, cooked sausage, bread, and cheese were offered frequently. Vegetables Mack had never seen, grown by Vietnamese farmers, were abundant. Everywhere the scent of dill filled the air. It was pickle time. Mack was gone longer than he should have been, so Ben and Roy were busy when he got back.

"I thought you were along to help," Ben growled, handing him a cloth nail apron filled with change.

Mack put it on and waited on a customer. Then another and another. From then on, he was so busy selling and packaging that everything around him was a constant motion without definition.

Suddenly, they were running out of vegetables to sell and the crowd was rapidly thinning. When the last of the vegetables were on the tables and most of the customers gone, Ben gave what was left to anyone who looked as though they could use it. All they loaded up to go home were empty boxes and crates.

"I think," Ben said, "I'll miss this place."

Mack knew Ben would miss a lot more than the market, and so would he. Even though he was away so many years, he grew up being part of the farm and the market, and they were part of him. Now, like the bull riding, it was about to disappear. How he longed for one more season, for one more good bull ride. One last ride.

He was silent, keeping his thoughts to himself, and feeling empty, lonely, almost lost. There was nothing he could do, he decided as he got in Roy's truck, except learn to live with it.

As they started out of the stall, a car drove up, stopping in front of them and blocking their way. Mandy got out and waved.

"Didn't think she'd make it," Roy said.

"You knew she was coming?"

"Yup, but she asked us not to say so. Wanted it to be a surprise."

"It is that," Mack said, then quickly left the truck and got into her car.

She waved to Roy and drove away without saying a word to Mack. They were on the freeway before she did.

"We have to hurry," she said. "I worked this morning. I'm still supposed to be there."

"Hurry what?"

"You'll see."

Mack hated mysteries. He didn't say anything because she was having fun, and he didn't want to spoil it for her. It wasn't long before he found out where they were going. She left the freeway and drove directly to the parking lot of a fancy suburban hotel. He thought she was stopping for an errand, so he stayed in the car.

"Mack," she laughed, "don't you want to go inside?"

"What for? I can wait here for you."
"It will work out much better if you come along."
"What do you mean? What will work better?"
"There's a room inside waiting for us. I don't have a lot of time."
"Is that what you meant about hurrying?"
"Yes."

Chapter 23

They were still on the highway, three miles from their turn-off and running in the left lane, when the late-model sedan pulled up next to Roy's right side. It slowed and a fat man peered through his open rear window into the passenger side of Roy's truck. He wasn't paying enough attention to notice what the fat man was holding on his stomach.

The car moved ahead, slowing again as it reached Ben's truck. The fat man poked something out of his open window, and Roy realized it was a gun. Either a rifle or a shotgun. Roy instantly dropped down from fifth to fourth gear and slammed his foot down hard on the accelerator. The four-hundred-plus horsepower engine, which he installed when he restored the one-ton truck, leaped to life. In an instant, he was on the sedan's bumper and, holding the pedal to the floor, rammed the rear of the car, hard.

It jumped ahead on impact, swerving wildly. The blast from the shotgun went over the hood of Ben's truck, with only a few pellets skittering across it, lightly scratching the faded paint. The car accelerated rapidly, and Roy let it go, his concern for Ben too great to go after it. He flagged him over, and they stopped along the highway on the left shoulder, partially blocking the left lane.

"You okay?" Roy asked when they were out of the trucks.

"I'm fine. What the hell is going on?"

"Don't know. Some asshole was in the back of that car. I didn't pay any attention to him when it slowed down going by me. When it got alongside of you, I saw the shotgun he had poking out the window. We're lucky this old buggy of mine has all those horses under the hood or you might not be looking so good right now."

"I don't know, Roy. He still had enough time to shoot quicker than he did. Unless it wasn't me he was trying to kill."

"Who the hell was he after then?"

"Mack. You said he slowed down going by you. What else would he be looking for? He could've taken a shot at either one of us right off, if he wanted to."

"Yeah, you're right. Mack's been nosing around a lot lately. I think he might've stuck his nose into some damn thing or another that's got someone worried about him. This little incident tells me that those shots fired the other day were no accident. There's no way I can believe they came from a poacher."

"I don't think so, either. I do for damn sure think we'd better find out who it is gunning for him. It's bad enough I'm losing my farm because of that project. I don't want to lose my boy too."

"You know I feel the same, Ben. He gets hurt, and someone's going to pay."

"You're right, payment is due. But we'd best get on home now."

"Yeah, let's roll. I want to clean and load the guns. It'll be a good idea to be ready, no matter what happens next."

"Good idea, Roy. If there's going to be any killing, it's better them dead than Mack."

Chapter 24

Mack showered as soon as they got into the room. Mandy was in bed, waiting for him when he came out, with only a sheet covering her. He got in next to her, kissing her as his hands moved over her body, wanting to touch all of her at once.

"Don't wait," she said, pulling him over her, "I want you now."

It surprised him. Years before, she had always demanded a lot of touching and time, constantly reminding him in the way she moved and responded that he must go slowly. This time was different, and it happened fast. Almost instantly for her, then again and again. He tried to slow it down to make it last. She wouldn't allow it. Far sooner than he wanted it to happen, he flew over the edge. He stayed with her for a moment and then he was gone again, soaring into space. When the flight ended, he moved off her and held her.

"I'm sorry," she said, "for hurrying it that way."

"It's okay. It was great, just not like I remember you."

"I couldn't wait. I've wanted you for so long. I've needed it for too long."

"It was fine for the first time."

"This for sure wasn't our first time, Mack. We used to spend a lot of time in bed."

"In this life, it was our first time. This is a brand-new life we have now."

"I love you, Mack."

"I love you too, Mandy."

They lay together for a short time, then she was in the shower and out, and they were on the way home. All doubts about how they felt about each other or what they were going to do were gone. Their only disagreement was on how soon. They talked about it on the way home.

"What I think we should do, Mandy," Mack told her, "is go to your house right now, pick up what you need, and get you the hell out of there…permanently. I don't want you getting hurt again."

"I can't. Not yet. Jason's got control of everything. All the money we've invested. Even the checking account, which is in his name at his bank. I don't even know for sure what our assets are. I have to get into his computer to find out. Otherwise, I could lose it all."

"So what?"

"Damn it, Mack, I've spent too much time with him to give up everything. Besides, it will be a lot easier for us to start our new life if we have it."

"I'm not looking for easy. We'll do okay. We don't need his money. I don't want his money."

"That's not the point."

"What is the point then?"

"It's my money too. Marriage is a partnership or it's supposed to be. I've worked awfully hard to get what we have. The only time I didn't work is after we lost the baby."

"About that, Mandy, I've been meaning to tell you how sorry I am. It must have been real hard for you."

"It was. A lot harder than it needed to be."

"What do you mean?"

"Jason. He blamed me. He said I didn't take care of myself properly while I was pregnant. He also said we were being punished by God because I didn't have enough faith."

"The jerk. He uses his faith crap a lot, doesn't he?"

"All the time. He says it's why your dad is losing the farm. That if his faith was strong enough, it never would've happened to him."

"If that's true, Jason's god is as big an asshole as he is."

"Mack! How can you say or even think such a thing about God?"

"I can say and think anything I want to about Jason's god. The creator, if there is one, isn't likely to waste any time with such stupid and childish nonsense. Do you really believe that an entity great enough to create this beautiful Mother Earth, not to mention the universe, is going to play such petty mind games? I think it's highly unlikely."

"How am I supposed to answer that, Mack? I've never thought about it the way you do. I never think about it much at all. I simply accept what I was taught."

"I've thought about it since I was a kid. I haven't believed for a long time. Now I think most of it's nothing more than a childish myth."

"Humans need to have spiritual beliefs. They need something to lean on. Not everyone is like you, you know."

"I never said anything about spiritual beliefs. I was talking about religion, theology to be exact. And if a person has any real spiritual beliefs, they'll have a strong reverence for life. Not only for human life but for all life and life forms. A belief that all creatures should be treated with dignity and respect. Without any crap about humans being the only creatures with an immortal soul. That's quite a contrast from ripping up a wildlife refuge, only to build a big playground for rich folk."

"That's silly, Mack. There are probably hundreds or even thousands of things about modern life that wouldn't work if we all tried to live your way."

"Maybe not. The thing is, if we continue to be hell bent on the destruction of planet earth, which is the only home we have, we're going to lose a lot more than our modern way of life. Our species is going to die."

"You're back to the project again, aren't you?"

"It's only one very small example of what we're doing. If people cared, there'd be riots before Jason and company could ever get it started."

"I love you, Mack, and I do care about all the things you're so passionate about. I guess I just don't understand all of it. When the current mess we're in is over, I promise I'll try to take the time to understand it better."

"Okay, Mandy, when we have more time."

Chapter 25

The instant Mack was out of the car, Mandy was off down the road, leaving a cloud of dust behind her. He wasn't sure whether she didn't see the car parked near the house or didn't take the time to mention it. Either way, he was glad she hadn't said anything. He wasn't up to explaining why Wanda was there.

She was inside, sitting at the kitchen table, talking and laughing with Ben and Roy. They ignored him when he went in. Ben even let him pour his own coffee. It didn't take any effort to see they liked her.

"Hi, Mack," she said as he sat down. "How's it going?"

"Fine. What's up?"

"Nothing special. I thought I'd stop by and say hello. See if you're busy this afternoon. I hope you don't mind. Ben said last night he thought it'd be okay."

"Of course it is. I'm not busy either, only real tired. There isn't anything I can think of that tires me out like the market does."

"Should I come back later after you get some sleep?"

"There's no need for that, Wanda," Ben said. "Roy and I will keep you company while the kid sleeps."

"What about you guys? Aren't you tired?"

"We're both too old," Roy said, "to sleep in the afternoon."

"Okay. Is it all right with you, Mack, if I wait here while you take a nap?"

"It sure is. I won't be more than an hour or two."

Mack went upstairs to bed. The last thing he heard before falling asleep was their laughter.

He felt like he was a short time from a bad bull ride when he woke up. He sat up slowly in the dark room, knowing he'd slept a lot longer than he planned. He hurt all over, his body racked by a constant, telling pain, brought on by loading and unloading the trucks and the long hours at the market standing on concrete. Each step he took going down the stairs reminded him of the toll his efforts had taken.

Other than a light on in the kitchen, the house was dark and empty. It was too early for Roy and Ben to be in bed, so he looked outside. Wanda's car was still there. Roy's truck was gone. He poured a mug of coffee from the pot left warming on the stove, then sat down at the table. He finished the mug of burnt to bitter coffee before he was awake enough to notice the note propped up in the middle of the table. It told him where they went and how long they'd be there, inviting him to join them if he was awake early enough and felt up to it. It said the keys to Wanda's car were in it.

Mack wasn't in the mood to go to a bar, so he sat in the living room with a good book until they got home. Ben invited Wanda in for coffee, then he and Roy discreetly disappeared. Mack knew she wanted to stay up and talk, but he was so tired by then, he could barely hold his eyes open. Too much market and too much pain had wiped him out.

She could see it and took him upstairs. He flopped on the bed and was quickly asleep. Right after, she said, "We'll talk tomorrow."

Mack woke up late and got out of bed slowly. His muscles were still sore, but the deep-down pain was less. His thoughts turned to Mandy, and he was thinking about her when he went downstairs. So it was a shock to see Wanda sitting at the kitchen table. She was wearing an old bathrobe Ben found for her the night before.

"'Morning," she said as he poured a cup of coffee.

"Good morning. You been up long?"

"About an hour. I've been too lazy to get dressed."

"It was a late night."

"Yes," she grinned, "just not late enough."

"I guess." He knew what she was leading up to and hoped to avoid it. He felt listless and unable to handle her comments.

"You don't sound like you agree, Mack."

"That's not it, exactly."

"What is it…exactly?"

"Me. I made a commitment and I'm sticking with it."

"Mandy, you mean."

"Yes."

"It figures."

"Is that all you've got to say?"

"That's not all I have to say, but saying anything else doesn't make any sense. Except…ah hell, forget it."

"I think you should say whatever it was you were going to say. Maybe you'll feel better."

"No, Mack, I won't feel better." She looked him in the eyes. He could see the hurt in hers, she could see the sorry in his. "It's too bad we didn't meet in another time. Maybe you and I would've worked." She pushed her chair away from the table and stood. "I think I have the ambition to get dressed now."

She left the kitchen. Mack heard the shower start and listened to it run for a long time. She was dressed when she came back.

"Good luck, Mack," she said, heading straight to the door.

"There isn't any reason for you to hurry out of here," he said, hoping she'd stay. It felt good to have her there, even if all they shared was friendship.

"I'd stay, if staying might bring me something I don't have. I know it won't and I hurt enough already."

"I know you hurt. I'm really sorry, but I still want to be friends, Wanda, if the time ever comes you think we can be."

"I don't know. Maybe sometime." She started out the door, then turned toward him again. "You know, Mack, I surely wish to God that I didn't love you."

He didn't mind what she said so much. He had it coming and knew it. It was her crying that bothered him.

Mack went out behind her, feeling low as he watched her drive away, wishing there was a way to lessen her pain and that he'd been more careful. He waited until she left the driveway, then joined Ben and Roy, who were again working on old machinery.

"You look down, Mack," Ben said, sensing his mood.

"Yeah. I just hurt Wanda. It was stupid of me, and it sure doesn't make me feel like much of a man right now."

"Something tells me you did as bad to yourself as you did to her. It was lousy timing too because there's something Roy and I have to tell you that can't wait. You aren't going to like it one bit either."

"More bad news?"

"Worse than bad."

Roy told him what happened on the highway on their way home from the market.

Ben finished Roy's story with "What happened yesterday has us wondering about those shots fired at you the other day. It doesn't seem so likely now that it was an accident."

"You think whoever it was yesterday was looking for me."

"It sure seemed like they were."

"I hate to admit it," Mack said, "but I think you're right. The shit never stops."

"Doesn't seem to."

Mack suddenly thought about Wanda again. She'd been seen all over town with him. Could she be in any danger? He couldn't take the chance.

"Roy, can I use your truck?"

"Why? It might be best if you hang around here. If someone is gunning for you, they know my truck."

"They know Wanda's car too."

"I'll drive. Coming, Ben?"

"No. Too crowded. You can handle it. Now git."

"Seat belt," Roy said as they got into the truck.

Roy handled the truck the way he did everything else, seemingly without effort. His fluid touch on the steering wheel kept the truck moving a steady ninety on the narrow, curving, gravel road. They caught Wanda on the next county road, poking along. Roy roared alongside her, with Mack waving for her to pull over. She did so reluctantly.

"Look," Mack told her when he got out of the truck, "I know you're upset and angry. I don't blame you one bit. The thing is..."

When he finished explaining why they were there, she let him drive her home, promising she'd be careful about what she did and where she went. By the time they got to her apartment, they were friends again. Mack was almost glad they had a reason to chase her.

Chapter 26

The auctioneer came to see Ben on Monday morning, bringing three hay wagons with him.

"These," he explained, "are for all the miscellaneous merchandise you have to sell."

What he really meant was junk. The favorite of most people who regularly attend country auctions are the wagons filled with boxes of god knows what, hoping they'll buy one with a hidden treasure in it. And it actually does happen occasionally. Most of it goes so cheap that if they find something worth ten dollars, they feel they've done well. It's also often true that what one person considers junk, someone else considers a treasure.

Collectors—and people will collect almost anything—are the best treasure hunters and the best spenders at most estate-type auctions. Antique and flea market dealers are only a short distance behind. Then there are the hoarders.

They want to buy as cheap as possible, haul home whatever it is they bought and put it in storage, be it a garage, shed, barn, or their house. Most of what they buy ends up at another auction, usually theirs, after they die. The bulk of the people at most estate auctions go because they like auctions. They're a social event. Sometimes they buy, sometimes they simply watch. Either way, they keep the food vendors in business.

Much of the equipment Ben used for farming came from auctions. It was thought to be junk by most people. To him, it was very usable equipment, only needing his capable hands to rebuild it. The money he'd saved by buying the farming machinery he needed at auctions was one of the reasons he managed to make a living so long on a small farm when most others couldn't.

The auctioneer walked around, checking on their progress, often nodding his approval at the work they were doing, and giving instructions on where he wanted everything put on auction day. He wanted to make it as easy as possible for the crowd to move along with him as he was selling, knowing that more people bidding meant more money for each item. He also knew he needed to move fast, to keep the crowd interested and somewhat anxious. Nothing kills the urge to spend as quickly as boredom.

When everything was looked over and instructions given, the auctioneer looked around, took off his cap to scratch his head, and said, "You've got a lot of stuff here, Ben. A lot more than I thought there was the first time I was here to make the list for the auction bill. Is there more I don't know about?"

"Just the junk in the sheds," Ben said. "I guess there's more up in the hayloft. I don't know exactly what's there yet. Most of it was here when I bought this place. I've never taken the time to see what it all was."

"Well, hell, Ben, you'd best get it out, so we know. It could be that some of it's worth some real money."

"It's nothing except junk, I'd guess."

"Maybe, maybe not. People are crazy for antiques. You could have a gold mine here."

"The attic's full too," Mack told him. "What's in it?"

"Don't know," Ben said. "It was full when we bought the place. Never saw any reason to clean it out after my wife died."

"For God's sake, man, clean it out now. How old is this farm?"

"Little over a hundred years."

"Get it hauled out, Ben. All of it, no matter what it is or where it is. Don't throw away a damn thing. I mean nothing! Not until I come back to look at it near the end of the week."

"Yes, sir," Ben agreed.

After he left, Ben went to work on the last of the machinery while Mack and Roy started organizing. The wagons were lined up end to end in the yard. Machinery was moved out into the field closest to the house and placed in neat rows according to what it was.

The antique machines were in front, followed by the machines still operational, with the junk machinery last.

With that done, Ben and Roy began emptying the barn's hayloft, and Mack worked on the sheds. The first thing he brought out was the old saddle Roy gave him with his first horse. It was worn and scuffed, but it was well made.

Mack cleaned and oiled it regularly when he used it, so it still had a lot of life left in it. Next, he hauled out an old harness. Its tarnished silver trim was still intact, although its leather was rotting away. Following it was an assortment of rusty chicken and pig feeders and a lot of miscellaneous cow milking equipment, including a cream separator and a butter churn. All of it was there when Ben bought the place.

A lot of what was left in the shed was scrap metal, old wooden boxes, and some beat-up furniture. Even an old icebox. Buried in a corner, Mack found a blacksmith's anvil. With the exception of some surface rust, it was in excellent condition. It was so heavy, it took two of them to carry it out. The last to come out of the shed was a couple of old egg crates filled with blacksmith's tools.

They knew the blacksmith equipment was valuable, so Mack took the time to clean it and paint it with stove black, making it look as though it was almost new. They found a large oak log about three feet long and two feet in diameter, which had been cut for firewood but wasn't yet split, that they stood on end. The anvil was set on it, and they hung the various hammers, tongs, and punches around it. It was an impressive sight. While Mack and Roy were working with the anvil and tools, Ben found a portable metal forge in another shed. It was about the size of a large charcoal grill, with a hand-cranked fan serving as a bellows. The fan was rusted tight, so they gave it a liberal dose of penetrating oil and pried it loose with a screwdriver. It too was cleaned and painted with stove black.

"Anyone who wants those," Roy said, "is going to pay plenty for them. Otherwise, I'm going to own them. They're in a lot better shape than what I'm using on my ranch now."

"The hell with that, Roy," Ben said, "if you want them, you take them."

"Not this time, Ben. This time, I buy what I want at the auction, the same as everyone else. Tools like those on the auction bill will bring a crowd. Crowds bring money."

"That's true. Still, if you want it..."

"Don't even think it, Ben."

It wasn't long before they were putting the things they considered antiques on the wagons and piling the rest on the ground. By midafternoon, Ben called the auctioneer to see if he could bring more wagons.

"How many more do you think you'll need, Ben?" he asked.

"Ten, fifteen, maybe twenty. Hard to say. We've still got three sheds, half the hayloft, the lower level of the barn, and the attic in the house to go. Not to mention my stuff, which is more than one man should own."

Ben told him all that they'd found.

"I'll be out tonight. You keep going. I'll bring tarps to cover the stuff. Don't worry about the personal things in the house. If I'm guessing right, and you continue to find the kind of things you have so far, you might not need to sell any of them."

A short time after Ben made the phone call, Mandy stopped by. Mack was almost as surprised to see her as he was by all the things they were finding tucked away in the farm's dark corners. And they'd barely started with what they originally thought would only take a day.

"You sure look like you've been busy," she said. "Where did all this stuff come from?"

"From all over around here. Most of it was here when Dad bought the place. My mother was going to go through it all. She got sick before she had the chance. After she died, we never saw any need to do it. There's a lot more left to dig out. So what brings you here this time of day? You take the day off?"

"I left work early."

"What's up?"

"Nothing special. Jason's out of town. Something to do with the project. It seemed like a good time to stop by and say hello. I didn't know you'd be so busy."

"It doesn't matter. How long will he be gone?"

"He said until tomorrow. That doesn't mean he will. He often comes back from his trips early. Mostly to check up on me, I'm sure. And this afternoon will be a good time to start digging into his computer."

"Be careful."

"I will."

Ben and Roy came out of the barn, lugging a large wooden chest. They were breathing heavily, and grunted as they set it on a wagon. Roy opened it, motioning for Mack and Mandy to take a look. It was full of compartments, trays, and boxes, each one holding a carpenter's hand tool. Saws, hammers, planes of all types and sizes, chisels, and dozens of other tools filled it. Everything was at least fifty years old. Because of the unique design of the chest, it was all in close to perfect condition.

"I think I'll go home," Mandy said. "You've got too much to do for me to be hanging around here, getting in the way. Mack, if Jason doesn't come home tonight, I'm taking tomorrow off. I'll be over in the morning to help. I think you guys need it."

"It would be greatly appreciated," Roy said.

"I think it's going to take the rest of the week to get ready for the auction Sunday," Ben said.

They went back to work, carrying and dragging an endless array of old farm equipment, tools, and furniture from the buildings. They didn't stop to eat until early evening, then took the time to drink a couple of beers to settle the hot dish Ben threw together. The auctioneer got there while they were enjoying their second beer. He had five more wagons with him.

"This is all I could round up today, Ben," he explained. "I don't think I should bring any more than this anyway. Make the yard too crowded during the auction. I'll have someone here to help you fill the wagons as they're emptied. If you keep all the excess neatly piled in the barn, it'll go okay. I've done it before at other big auctions. Now, all the furniture you have scattered around or find anywhere, put under cover. Pieces like that old icebox you left laying out by that shed are almost as valuable as anything else you've found. Anything you come across that water will damage should be kept under cover. Even old pictures, photographs, magazines, papers, those types of things. It's all worth money, and a lot of it's going to bring in big money, so handle it carefully. And for god's sake, please keep it all dry!"

"What should we put on the wagons first?"

"Whatever you think is worth the most money. Antiques, fancy glassware, pottery. Whatever you find that looks valuable."

"Isn't that kind of backward from the way it's usually done?"

"Yes. Deal is, with an auction this size, I think it'll be best to sell the highest dollar merchandise first. By the time we get through all this, it'll be getting late and the crowd will be thinning considerably. Let's get the real money from them while they're here. If we sell the high-buck things with a good crowd, the things that are really junk won't matter. The amount of money they bring in will be insignificant either way."

"Do you really think," Ben asked, "it makes a difference how you sell any of it? It's all junk."

"No, it isn't. It's my guess there's more money here than you're going to need. If the rest of what you haven't brought out yet looks as good as what you've found so far, we might be able to skip selling the real estate as well as your personal things."

"You are kidding?"

"Not at all. I think this is going to prove to be the best auction I've ever had the privilege to conduct."

"Be damned. It's just junk."

The auctioneer laughed. "Ben, it ain't. I'll be back tomorrow evening. See where we stand. Now I've got to get out of here. I'm going to talk to the radio station about some ads, then see if the printer can get me some new auction bills printed up tomorrow."

"All that for some junk?"

"Ben!"

"Yeah, I know, all this junk ain't junk."

"You've finally got the idea, Ben. You do what I say, and I doubt very much you're going to lose this farm."

CHAPTER 27

The clouds rolled in an hour after sunup. A short time later, the rain started. It dropped straight down without any wind, thunder, or lightning. Only a dull gray mist, chilling the air and bringing memories of the fall and winter, which always seem to come too early in Minnesota. Mack, Ben, and Roy spent their early morning hours covering what they could with tarps and moving the rest they wanted to keep dry into the barn.

"This is the last thing we needed," Ben said when they were done. "We can't hardly dig any more out of the sheds now."

"Why don't we start going through the attic?" Mack suggested. "We can sort it in the house, then haul it out when it stops raining."

"It's going to make a hell of a mess," Ben complained. "Nothing we can't clean up after."

"True. Let's get at it then."

They carried several boxes out of the attic and down to the living room, then sat down, sorting the contents as they went through them.

"Look at this crap," Ben complained as soon as they started working. "Nothing but junk." He lifted a handful of very old valentines. "Who the hell would ever want these? We ought to haul all of it out and burn it. Be a good day for a fire, wet as it is."

"Ben," Roy said slowly, clearly, to make his point, "we know how working with this frustrates you. It isn't what you might call fun. So I've got to show you something about this so called junk. Give me those things a minute."

Ben handed the valentines to Roy, and he opened the top card. A heart popped up as he did. The words "I love you" were cut into it, with small hearts cut all the way around it, making it look more like a delicate piece of lace than paper.

"This one piece of junk I've got here, Ben," Roy explained, "will bring maybe twenty, twenty-five dollars at an antique store. I've got ten, fifteen more in my hand, and I'd guess you've got at least a hundred more in the box. If somebody's at the auction who really wants these, they could bid as high as two hundred for the box. They'll bring even more if we split them up into cardboard trays or something. If you believe two hundred dollars is no more than junk, maybe you ought to go somewhere else. Mack and I will have this auction and split the profits with you when it's done."

"Still looks like junk to me."

"Ben, if it isn't a tool you need to farm or a book to read, to you, it isn't worth a thing. Not every fool in the world is a farmer and most fools don't read. You've got a gold mine here, whether you think it is or isn't. So stop your incessant complaining."

They worked for a while, until it became obvious they didn't have enough boxes, and most of them were too large to be auction boxes.

"It's not hard to see," Roy said, "that one of us best go to town and pick up some boxes. Isn't difficult to know who it ought to be either since he's been grumbling about one thing or another all morning."

"Be a pleasure," Ben said, standing, "to get the hell away from all this dust and junk. What kind of boxes you want?"

"Whatever you can get. Stop at the liquor store first. Get as many of those trays canned beer comes in as you can."

"What for? They don't hold enough. They'll only take up a lot of room with nothing in them. Be a week doing the auction that way."

"It doesn't matter if it takes a week or a month, Ben. Get them anyway. Now get the hell out of here before Mack and I are so tired of your bitching, we go find us a nice quiet bar to spend this rainy day in."

"Oh sure, Roy, you're so old a day of drinking would kill you, you old fool."

"I'll never be too old for anything, Ben. Now get out of here. Go blow the stink off."

By now, both Ben and Roy were half smiling, and Mack knew they were releasing some of their tension. He wisely buried his head in the box he was sorting through and kept his mouth shut. By the time Ben left for town, the living room floor was covered with a wide assortment of old jewelry and jewelry boxes, various types of greeting cards, and old magazines, going as far back as the twenties. There were dozens of old tins of all types. Most of them were advertising tins, which were worth the most money. They'd found boxes of antique kitchen utensils; a shoe box of letters sent by a man while serving in the Civil War; hundreds of old photographs; catalogs going back to the turn of the century; and an odd assortment of vases, pottery, china, and glassware.

"You got any idea what we got here, Mack?" Roy asked.

"Enough so I'm fairly sure Dad will be in decent financial shape when the auction's over."

"It'll be a lot better than decent. He for sure isn't going be selling this farm."

"It's worth that much?"

"There's furniture in the back of the attic. From what I can see, it's all in pretty good shape. I think he's not only going to be able to pay off everything he owes, along with the note on this farm, he'll have enough left to keep on farming a few more years. It's a blessing he never got around to cleaning out the attic. Back when he bought this farm, a lot of this stuff wasn't worth much. Some of it wasn't worth anything. Now it's all considered antiques or, at the very least, collectibles. Hell, we found a buried treasure up there."

"But the farm is supposed to sell at noon on auction day."

"The auctioneer and I already decided to keep a tally going. We take in enough money, we'll cancel the sale of the farm. By then, Ben can't argue."

"Will there actually be enough money brought in that early in the auction?"

"We'll know by then if there's going to be enough."

"Won't a lot of people get upset if we cancel the sale of the farm after the auction's started?"

"Mostly, it'll only be the bank's people. If the farm gets sold, they'll be the ones who buy it."

A short time later, Mandy arrived.

"I didn't think you were coming today," Mack said, "when it got so late."

"I was up most of the night," she said. "I got into Jason's computer, finally. I don't know how I did it, but I erased one of the files when I was copying them. I spent most of the night trying to get it back."

"You can't go back there again, Mandy. You know what he'll do when he finds out."

"It doesn't matter, I still have to go back."

"Did you find out what he's been doing?"

"Some of it. I know he moved a lot of money around for quite a while, then put it all into one stock. A company called Lands Magnificent."

"Never heard of it."

"Neither have I."

"I wonder if it's the corporation behind the project?"

"I wouldn't doubt it. It sure would explain why Jason's put so much time into it. I don't think he'd be so dedicated if it didn't involve his own money."

"I still don't like the idea of you going back."

"I have to, Mack. Now let me look at all this wonderful stuff. Is this what you found in the attic?"

"It's the start of it. We're bringing it down a little at a time."

"You've got to be kidding. There's more?"

"Lots more. The attic's full, and it covers the whole third floor."

"Wow," she said, sifting through the jewelry, "this is going to be a fun auction."

Within ten minutes, they had another visitor. It was Wanda. Mack felt a hard knot grow in his stomach the instant he saw her. How could he possibly explain her to Mandy? She merely laughed when he, red-faced and nervous, led Wanda into the living room to make the introductions.

"Like I told you before, Mack," Wanda said, "we already know each other. We do live in a small town, you know."

"So what brings us the pleasure of your company today, Wanda?" Roy asked.

"A hell of a lot of curiosity. There's rumors flying all over town about this auction you're having. Seems like almost everyone I waited on at the cafe this morning was talking about it. It's been on the radio since last night. I left work early to check it out. From the looks of what I see here, it's going to be even better than it sounded."

"You've got to come over here," Mandy told her, "and look at this old jewelry. It's fantastic. A lot of it was made with real gemstones."

Mandy and Wanda were finished with the jewelry and going through the valentines when Ben got back. He motioned for Mack and Roy to leave the room.

"I got all the boxes I could find in town," he said. "The manager at the liquor store said he'd save me all I want if I pick them up every day. It was something, the questions I got asked about this junk auction."

"What else have you got to tell us, Ben?" Roy asked. "You look upset."

"I know who was shooting at us Saturday on our way back from market. I saw him in town. Surprised I didn't know right away who he was, dark glasses or not."

"Who is it?"

"The damn sheriff! Don't that beat all?"

"It might," Roy said, "if I didn't live in Texas."

"This ain't Texas, Roy," Ben said. "Here, it's the sheriff we call when we got trouble. Who do we call now when we've got problems?"

"I think I know," Mack said, then told them about deputy Dale Magee and what he suspected.

"It means Jason's involved in all this, Mack," Roy said. "You really think they killed that manager?"

"I think there's a good chance of it. Did either one of you get a look at the driver of the car?"

"It was a female," Roy said. "Dark hair, black maybe, and short. A decent looker."

"What little description that is, it fits Elaine. She works at the refuge. Dale's seen her meeting with Jason and the sheriff."

Mandy and Wanda joined the men in the kitchen.

"If you wanted to keep this conversation a secret," Mandy said, "you should learn to keep your voices down."

"So you think Jason and the sheriff," Wanda said, "were involved in Ray's murder?"

"Elaine too."

"Elaine's involvement I don't doubt," Wanda said. "She's a real bitch."

"How do you know that?" Mack asked, surprised at the intense dislike in her voice.

"Her and Rich come in for breakfast quite a bit. She's always giving me hell for being too long bringing the coffee or some damn thing."

"Her and Rich?" Mandy asked.

"Yes, her husband."

"He works at the refuge too, right?"

"He does," Mack explained. "He's been there for a long time. A hell of a nice guy, actually."

"You know Rich very well?" Ben asked Wanda.

"Only as a customer." Wanda answered. "I know his first wife died about three years ago. Cancer, I think. He married Elaine a little over a year ago."

"Wait a minute," Mandy interrupted. "I want to make sure I'm following all this. You guys think Jason, the sheriff, and this Elaine person murdered the manager of the refuge and now want to kill Mack. That's kind of far-fetched isn't it? It doesn't make sense."

"I think," Mack said, "Jason is capable of anything when it involves money. We need to find out about this Lands Magnificent Company. If it's the company behind the project, it ties it all together."

"My god!" Mandy said, shock written across her face, "It's still hard to believe Jason would kill for money!"

"And you live with him." Mack said. "Time to get out, Mandy. Now!"

"All I can say, Mandy," Ben said, "is that Mack's right. We've got room. Stay here, we'll get this auction done, then Mack, Roy, and I will get you moved somewhere. Neither Jason nor the sheriff are big enough to stop the three of us from doing it."

"It's time to quit kidding yourself, Mandy," Roy added. "Twice that we know of, they've tried to kill Mack. The son of a bitch you're married to is no good. Never was. You ought to know that."

"I don't think I should stay here anyway. It wouldn't look right. The divorce is going to be hard enough without Jason having that to use against me."

"Looking right isn't what's important. Staying alive is."

"He wouldn't kill me."

"No?" Roy asked.

"Look, you guys," Wanda said, "in a lot of ways, Mandy's right. If she ends up in divorce court, staying here could hurt her. Do you want to stay with me, Mandy? My place is nothing fancy, but it's big enough. We're close to the same size, and I have enough clothes to get you through the week. All of us will get you moved next week, after the auction."

"Mack?" Mandy asked, her eyes pleading.

"I don't like it, but okay, as long as you promise me you'll be careful and that if Jason comes around, you'll call Dale and me, right after you call the town cops."

"All right. I can do that. And I wouldn't worry, Mack, if I were you, about what Wanda might tell me. Whatever it is, it's not going to bother me."

"All that's great," Ben said, "and I hope all of you are happy now. Thing is, we've got an auction to get ready for, so how about we do? Are you ready, Mack?"

"As I'm going to be."

"Me too," Roy said, in mock fear.

"Smart ass," Ben said with a grin, knowing they were going to go at it again.

Chapter 28

Jason slammed the receiver down hard, furious at Mandy. Who did she think she was? Not coming home! Staying at a girlfriend's? She was at Mack's most likely. No way would she get any money out of a divorce. None of this would've happened if Mack Thomas wasn't around. He should be dead now, along with his hillbilly wife.

All the trouble Ben caused was bad enough. Why were they interfering with his business, only to preserve a wasted piece of ground? They were stupid when they put the environment ahead of business. He wasn't going to allow them to continue.

Vengeance is mine, said the Lord, and Jason, like the Lord, intended to take his own revenge. The earth was put here to use. It was put here for people, not creatures and trees. How dare the ecology freaks try to damage a project that would make so much money? Not only for him. A few others would do well too. Business was what made the world work and kept the peons busy. Not animals or grass or clean air. He certainly didn't need any of those. If he wanted an animal, he'd buy a dog. He already had grass to mow and an air conditioner to keep his air clean.

Now they'd taken his wife away. He would definitely keep a tighter rein on her in the future. No more discipline with an open hand. From now on, he'd use the belt. She'd learn it was her duty to obey and provide the money for all household and car expenses, so he could continue making his investments.

It was time to make some calls and have a meeting to decide what to do about the auction. It must be stopped. The earth would go in a blaze of glory after the second coming. Maybe now was the time to start the fires. He called the sheriff first, then Elaine. Her husband answered the phone, so he hung up. She'd know who called and where to meet. Getting out was no problem for her. Rich was simply too stupid to ever catch on to anything. He was only another preservationist, spending his time worrying about the wasted and wasteful refuge. Jason left the house, got to the meeting place first, and was on his third drink when the sheriff and Elaine arrived.

"So what's this about?" Elaine asked as she sat down. "I hope it's important. I really stretched it to get out tonight."

"You can't even say hi?" Jason growled, the alcohol in his system rapidly making his bad mood worse.

"I haven't got time for it. Rich didn't like my leaving. He's getting suspicious. We stopped the environmental impact study he was working on with Ray, and we can't have Rich doing another one like it. So what's this meeting about?"

"Did you hear about the Thomas auction?"

"No, I was out in the field today with Rich because he's dragging his feet on the study. What about it?"

"Seems like," the sheriff said, not about to let Jason do all the talking, since he considered Elaine to be his woman, "Ben Thomas has come up with a mess of antiques to sell. Word is, it's going to bring in a lot of money. If he keeps his farm, it'll mean more delays, and the Lands Magnificent stock will go down again. I got everything I own tied up in it. If I have to sell it the way it is, I'm going to take a hell of a beating on it."

"We're all in the same boat," Elaine said. "So what're we going to do?"

"I think we should consider a fire." Jason said.

"It's not a problem," the sheriff said, grinning. "Jason and I know a couple of guys. They've been growing a lot of pot. Dealing some hard stuff too. They owe us more'n the cut we've been getting. They'll do it 'cause they ain't got no choice."

"How soon can you get it done?" Jason asked.

"Tonight'd be pushing it. Tomorrow night for sure."

"Have them burn it all. House, barn, sheds, wagons. All of it."

"No problem."

"Good. You going to have a drink with us, Elaine?"

"No she ain't, Jason. We got something to do. Ain't that right, kid?" He smiled the most lecherous smile he had.

"You bet. Let's go. I really am in a hurry."

The two went outside and got in the van, neither of them noticing the man in the car parked near them. Jason stayed inside and ordered another drink. In less than ten minutes, the sheriff was back. He waved at the waitress to bring him another drink as he sat down with Jason, a big smile on his face.

"I got to tell you, Jason," he said, "what that woman does is magic. No doubt about it, she's got talent."

You bet, Jason thought, *and you're jackass enough to think she does it for you.* He gave the sheriff a knowing smile.

"I ain't so stupid, Jason, that I don't know you want some of her too. I've seen you look at her like you want it, plenty of times. Thing is, I ever catch you messing with her, you ain't gonna like what I'll do."

"Really? What's that? Tell your wife on me?"

"You leave my wife out of this. She's a good, God-fearing woman. Ain't her fault she don't like sex."

"Whose is it?" Jason asked, feeling macho now. "Yours?"

"Listen, you son of a bitch. I can break you in half with one hand, and if you ain't careful, I will."

"No, you won't. You're in too deep and you're never going to get out. So back your fat ass off. I'll do what I want to do, when I want to do it, and you can't do a thing about it."

"Why you…"

"Why me nothing. Now finish your drink and go take care of business. There's more important things for you to do than worry about sharing your blowjobs. Money's where it's at, Elmer."

The sheriff glared at Jason, downed his drink, then left the bar. He paid no attention to the nearly empty parking lot and didn't notice the car that followed him out.

Jason waited until he was gone, then left the booth he was in and walked to a table where two young ladies sat down shortly before the sheriff left.

"Hello, Susan," he said, "mind if I join you?"

Susan smiled a knowing smile. "Of course not, Jason." She nodded toward her friend. "Jason, I'd like to have you meet my friend, Judy...Judy Geyer. She's up from the cities, visiting her folks this week."

"Hi, Jason," she said, "it's nice to meet you." But she thought, *What a liar I am. I don't want to know this jerk.*

Chapter 29

The rain was still falling in the morning, so they continued to empty the attic. Mack and Roy took it in stride, doing what needed to be done. Ben acted more like a caged bear, constantly complaining that a man shouldn't be cooped up in the house on a summer day.

"Damn it, Ben," Roy told him, "you ought to be near the happiest man alive after what the auctioneer said last night. Looks like you're going to keep this farm. What more do you want?"

"To be outside."

"So go outside. Finish bringing down the stuff in the hayloft."

"Can't. We've got to get this done."

"Mack and I'll do it. What's really bothering you?"

"Nothing, Roy. Not a damn thing."

"Spit it out, Ben, before you really irritate me."

"It's the auction, Roy. It isn't right. All I hear is how lucky I am to be getting all this money. It isn't my money. I didn't do anything to earn it. How can I feel good about it?"

"Whose money is it, Ben?"

"The folks who lived here before me, I guess."

"They're dead and they sold you this place. You've been paying for it with hard work for a lot of years."

"All I bought was this farm. Not all the junk that's supposed to make me so much money."

"You forget how upset you were when you moved in and they'd left this stuff. You asked them to come and get it. They said they bought it with the place and they were selling it with the place. So why does it bother you?"

"It doesn't seem right, a man getting so much for nothing. Seems like I ought to have worked for it."

"You did. What's really bothering you, Ben, is your Lutheran guilt. After all the years you've been working in those fields, there's no way you should feel guilty. You've earned every dime. If you use some sense, you're going to earn a whole lot more. Do some real good in the process too."

"How?"

"When this auction is done, I'll tell you all about it. If you settle down now."

"Okay. I think I'll take me a walk, look at the fields. See if the poison the county agent said was there has killed anything else."

Ben was out walking when Mandy and Wanda got there. They weren't expected, so Mack and Roy were surprised to see them.

"We're taking the rest of the week off," Mandy explained, "to help you guys. We wouldn't be so late if we hadn't stopped at Katie's. Some girl was killed last night. We stayed to find out who it was."

"Who was it?" Mack asked.

"She was from the cities. I guess she went out with a friend of hers last night. Someone who works at the bank."

"The name of the girl killed was Judy Geyer," Wanda said.

"How was she killed?" Roy asked. "Car accident?"

"She was murdered. Someone hit her on the back of the head with a pipe or something. They're not sure."

"I hate hearing about this kind of thing," Roy said. "There's probably some nut case running around."

"Damn!" Mack said, loudly.

They all turned their attention to him. He was pale and staring at the floor, shaking his head.

"What's going on, Mack?" Roy asked.

"I think the girl's murder might in some way be connected to what's going on around here."

"Why?" Roy asked. "How can the murder of someone, not connected to any of this, be connected?"

"Something I never told anyone. After I left the hospital, when I was on my way to the bus station, I was jumped. I pretty much forgot about it because I thought it was a mugger. Jason knew where I was and that I was coming home. Given all that's happened and because the mugger was trying to take me out with a tire iron, I've got to wonder."

"I guess we've all got to wonder," Roy said. "What can we do about it?"

"Not much. Let's forget it for now."

"So let's get to work helping you guys." Mandy said "You won't be ready for the auction unless we do."

"The hell," Roy said, "we'll get it done."

"Oh, you'll get it out and on the wagons, spread out every which way, covered with god knows how many years of grime. Well, that's not the way it's going to be done. Wanda and I are going to wash everything that needs washing, and then we'll sort all of it the right way."

"It ain't really necessary to—"

"Go find something to do, Roy."

"Damn stubborn women," Roy said, smiling as he walked away.

They started working and, with Mandy's direction, were quickly moving smoothly.

"What are you two doing here?" Ben asked when he came in a short time later.

"What needs doing, Ben, honey," Wanda said, reaching up and kissing his cheek, then running the tips of her fingers over it. "So why don't you carry this out to the barn." She pointed at a pile of trays filled with washed and sorted glassware. "On your way back, bring in all the dirty things you took out there yesterday."

Ben didn't argue, knowing he was beaten before he started.

The rest of the morning was filled with work. It was a steady process of moving, washing, and sorting. By noon, the rain stopped. Ben almost cheered, he was so anxious to work outside.

Wanda cooked dinner, and with most of the earlier tension gone, the meal was filled with laughter and teasing. Mack and Mandy sat close together but avoided any direct contact. Wanda flirted unmercifully, with Ben a little and with Roy a lot. It was midafternoon when Jason arrived. Roy was the first to see him. He stopped Jason as soon as he got out of his car.

"You want something?"

"I'm here to pick up my wife."

Roy blocked his way, glaring at him and not moving an inch. Jason tried to push him aside. Roy grabbed him by his tie, lifting the bigger man up and against his car, dusting it with the back of his fancy banker's suit.

"You're not going anywhere. You're not doing anything. And you will stay away from Mandy. You so much as breathe hard on her again, I'm going to bust you into little pieces and stomp on them. So don't even think about screwing with me!" He slammed Jason against the car, hard. "You understand me?"

Jason glared back, refusing to answer. Roy pushed him harder against the car, then slapped him twice across the face, leaving huge red welts on both cheeks.

"It's like this," Roy told him between clenched teeth, "I'd enjoy messing you up. So go ahead and give me an excuse."

"You do anything to me, and I'll have the law on you."

Roy slapped him again. "Who, your crooked sheriff friend? Tell that son of a bitch I'm looking for him." Roy dropped Jason, spun him around, pushed him, then kicked him with the pointed end of his cowboy boot. "Now get out of here while you can."

"I have a right to take Mandy!" Jason screamed.

Roy hit him, and he shriveled and dropped. By then, Ben and Mack were there, and Mandy and Wanda were on their way out of the house. They stood, staring at Roy while he went to the side of the house, got the garden hose, and sprayed cold water over Jason. Slowly, he came around.

Jason stood a moment, complete disbelief written on his face, then got in his car.

"You'll pay for this, Mandy!" he screamed as he backed out of the driveway.

"Wish you would have let me do that, Roy," Mack said.

"Now why should I be letting you have all the fun around here? I've wanted to do that since the first time I ever met the asshole."

"Why do you feel that way?" Mandy asked.

"Because Jason gets what he wants by using people, religion, and intimidation. Worst of all, he's lazy. Not to mention he beats on you and that I can't abide by at all. I think I can speak for Ben and Mack on that too."

Mandy fought back tears.

"I'm sorry, Mandy," Mack said, "for us being so hard."

"Oh, Mack," Mandy said, "don't apologize for what Roy said. He's right. I just can't believe you all care so much. I lived with him so long and let him do what he does. I'm almost as wrong as he is."

"No way," Roy said, his voice growing hard. "If you got to lay blame, Mandy, lay it on him and his greed, the way his mommy and daddy raised him, and that idiotic religion he's always throwing around."

"My god, Roy, he's a Lutheran!"

"Well now, Mandy, you just made my point exactly. When his like catch hold of it, it's all idiotic. It doesn't matter what name you put on it."

"You sound just like Mack."

Roy smiled. "No, Mandy, Mack sounds just like me."

Chapter 30

The only thing about getting older that bothered Roy much was the middle of the night call to the toilet. This night was no different than any other, and at 1:30, he woke up. As was his habit, he got up, used the bathroom, went downstairs to the kitchen, and poured himself a cup of coffee.

He sat down in the dark, lit a cigarette, and thought about the day's events, wondering what it was that drove men like Jason. He was dangerous Roy knew. But at least Mandy was somewhat safe now. They were able to convince her, this time, to leave her car at the farm when she went to Wanda's so Jason wouldn't find it and know she was staying in town. It was better for Wanda too. No telling what Jason would do to her, either. It was a certainty he'd blame everyone except himself for Mandy's leaving him. Jason wasn't the kind who could ever admit he was wrong.

Roy was smoking his second cigarette when he heard the truck outside. It came up without headlights and stopped away from the house. Two men got out quietly. One of them reached in the back of the pickup and took out a five-gallon gas can.

"What the hell are they up to?" Roy wondered.

His eyes were accustomed to the darkness because he'd been sitting with the lights off, so he moved easily to the front hall closet where the guns were kept. He chose a thirty-caliber lever action over the more powerful rifles with scopes. It's relatively short length made it easy to handle and fire. He slapped a loaded clip into it, worked the lever to load the rifle, grabbed two more clips with his left hand,

and crept out the seldom-used front door on the opposite side of the house from the two men.

They were working their way toward him, spilling gasoline onto the house. Roy moved into some bushes a short way out in the yard, hoping they'd move away from the house before he was forced to let them know he was there. He didn't want to do anything to light the gasoline they were dumping on it. He got lucky, and they moved all the way around the house, then toward the barn and other outbuildings, to douse them with gas before lighting any of the buildings. Roy followed them around, then stepped in the open when they were halfway between the barn and old chicken coop.

"That's far enough!" Roy yelled. "Drop the gas and lay down with your faces in the dirt."

The men looked at each other, then dropped the gasoline can. The empty-handed man yanked a small pistol from his belt and fired wildly at Roy, who dove headfirst on the ground, firing the rifle twice at them on his way down. His aim was way off. A bullet hit the gas can. It exploded, knocking the two men to the ground, drenching them with burning gasoline. They screamed.

Roy got up and ran toward them to try and help. They were completely engulfed in flames, too hot for him to get close. They were too far from the house for the hose to reach, so he filled a bucket with water and ran back to the fire. It did nothing to abate the flames, and they died before he could do anything else to save them.

The explosion woke Ben and Mack. As soon as he saw the flames, Mack rushed to the phone and called 911. Ben ran out to Roy.

"What the hell's going on?" he asked Roy, who was standing there with an empty pail in his hands, watching the flames eat away at the bodies of the dead men.

"A couple of total idiots got themselves burned alive," Roy answered, shaking his head and dropping the pail. "They were trying to burn you out. If it wasn't for my every night pee call, they'd have done it too. The bastards."

"You sure that's what they were doing?" Ben asked.

"Take a smell around the house. If I'd of hit that can of gas close to it, you and Mack would've likely burned up too. You call the fire department or cops yet?"

"Mack's doing it. Why would anyone want to burn me out?"

"To stop the auction, why else? I only hope Jason is one of those bastards laying over there, stinking up the yard. At least then I'll never have any doubts as to why they came here to kill us."

"I can't see Jason having the guts to do something like this on his own, Roy. Likely as not he hired them. He'd never dirty his own hands."

"You're right. Either way, they were stopped in time. It's better them dead than us."

"It is, but this has gotten way out of hand. I'm beginning to believe I should've sold this place when they wanted to buy it."

"No, Ben. You aren't selling anything now, either, except at the auction. After that, we'll see. I'm going to put on some clothes, then get the hose and wash the gasoline off the house."

Mack came out as Roy went in.

"What the hell happened?" Mack asked Ben.

"A couple of guys were here to burn us out. Took a shot at Roy. He shot back. Hit their gas can. It blew and they burned."

"Is Roy okay?"

"He's pissed. He's real pissed. Me too."

"He just killed two men. Doesn't it bother him?"

"They came here to burn us out and kill us. How's he supposed to feel?"

Mack went in the house to dress. Roy was spraying the house with the hose, and Mack and Ben were watching the last of the flames die down when the fire trucks drove in the yard. The firemen quickly put out the fire, then helped Roy wash the remaining gas off the house. Two sheriff's cars drove in then. Dale Magee was in the first and the sheriff in the second.

"Hello, Mack, Mr. Thomas," Dale said. "What happened here?"

"I'll ask the questions, Dale," the sheriff said, swaggering up to them. Ben told him what happened.

"You know, Thomas, it doesn't matter what you might of thought them fellows was doing, you can't be killing them."

"That so, Sheriff," Roy said, the rifle in his hands again.

"Better give me the gun," the sheriff said.

"Go to hell," Roy said. "You might be a cop, but this time you don't give orders."

"You can't talk to me that way," the sheriff said, stepping back and pulling out his pistol.

Roy slapped the gun out of his hand with the rifle butt, making a loud cracking sound. The sheriff grabbed his injured hand with his other one and moaned as he tried to squeeze the pain away.

"Those two burned-up pieces of garbage lying over there," Roy barked, "tried to burn us up in the house. Attempted murder is what it's called. I wasn't trying to kill them. I accidentally hit their gas can defending myself, after they fired on me. That's the reason they burned. It's simple enough for even you to understand, so back the hell off."

"There ain't no proof of that, and you'll be going to jail. Dale, go call more deputies."

Dale didn't move.

"What the hell you standing there for, Deputy? Do what you're told."

"Not this time, Elmer," Dale said quietly. "I know who owns the truck. Friends of yours, aren't they? I followed you last night when you went to see them, after you left your little meeting with Jason and the refuge lady. Now I know why you went. Other than to collect your share of the drug money that is. You went way too far this time, Elmer. Way too far."

"Okay, Mister Dumb Shit Sheriff," Roy said, "here's the way we're gonna do this. You'll write out your report exactly as I say. Turn it in tonight, and tomorrow, you'll decide you're getting too old to do such a dangerous job any longer. When you resign, you'll recommend this fine young man as your replacement until the next election. Then if you're smart, you'll run like hell before he's able to prove everything we know you're involved in."

"Like what? I didn't do anything wrong, no matter what Dale says. I've been a good cop."

"Sure you have. Like when you and Jason and I don't know who else killed the manager over at the refuge. Like trying to shoot us on the highway last Saturday. Like hiring the dead pukes over there to burn us out and like whatever else you've done. Now get out of here, fill out the reports the way I said, then resign. If I see you around me or mine again, I'm going to kill you. The best you can ever hope for now is to run like hell or go to jail."

"Can I take my gun with me?" the sheriff asked, his voice deflated.

"So long as you unload it first."

He did, then turned away like a man who's been thoroughly beaten, walked slowly to his car, and left. He went back to his office and filled out the reports the way Roy told him to. He included a glowing recommendation for Dale, saying he was by far the best deputy to fill his position until an election was held. He knew the county board would have no choice other than to follow his recommendation. Their only real concern was holding down the cost of law enforcement. There was no sense, he decided, to have anyone in the job that didn't know that Jason was involved in everything. He hated him too much to let him off easy. He didn't care if Elaine was caught or not. What little she'd given him had cost him a lot, but he still had mixed feelings about her.

He tried to call his wife. As he expected, she didn't answer the phone. She rarely did when he worked nights. He loaded his pistol, held it in his lap, staring at it while he wondered why it was she hadn't answered his call this time. Finding no answer to his question and knowing he wouldn't, he sighed heavily, closed his eyes, put the gun in his mouth, and pulled the trigger.

It never occurred to him to leave a note explaining why he did it.

CHAPTER 31

Dale called the support people he needed to clean up the charred corpses and gather the evidence necessary to verify Roy's story. He stayed after everyone else left.

"You got time to come in for a cup of coffee?" Ben asked.

"No, I don't. I'll take it anyway."

"So tell me, Dale Magee," Roy said when they were settled around the kitchen table, "are you going to be able to do anything about Jason and company now?"

"If you mean arrest him or the other two, no. We don't have any real proof of anything. We know, without a doubt, that the two who died tonight were trying to burn you out. We still can't prove yet that they were in any way connected to Jason. If they were alive..."

"Trouble is, shit happens when you get shot at."

"I understand. I'll keep working on it, Mr. Thomas."

"Dale, he's Ben and I'm Roy. The mister shit is for bankers and lawyers and other assholes."

"Okay, Roy."

"What can you do, Dale?" Mack asked.

"What I've been doing. A lot will depend on what the sheriff does. Even if he resigns and leaves, no doubt he's guilty, we'll still have to prove it."

"What about Jason and Elaine?"

"Same thing, we'll keep digging. I thought we might be able to hang Jason for spraying your crops, but when I traced it down and found the outfit that did the spraying, they were supposedly hired by a James Anderson. The bill was always paid with a certified check, written out of a bank in Minneapolis. It wasn't James Anderson who did it. He's a retired dairy farmer, lives over north of the refuge's western side, not far from Glentago. He was in the hospital most of the summer. Had a heart attack and damn near died. His son runs their farm now. Someone used his name. He and his son bank in Kingsburg at Jason's bank. That ought to tell you who that someone is. The only thing you can do about it now is sue the company who did the actual spraying."

"Hell of a lot of good that'll do," Ben said. "They were stupid and sloppy, doing business that way. It doesn't make them guilty of a crime."

"No, it doesn't," Dale agreed. "I'm just sorry it didn't get us any closer to hanging Jason and Elaine."

"This Elaine," Mack said, "is married to my friend Rich. Do you think it would be okay after the auction if I pay him another informal visit?"

"As long as you're careful. I'd prefer none of them know for sure how much we know. I'd also prefer that you don't get yourself hurt or killed."

"I'll be careful. I won't push it too hard."

"Good. I'm certain we'll get them, sooner or later."

"I'd feel a lot better if it was sooner. With Jason around, I worry a lot about Mandy."

"Mandy?"

"She's Jason's wife..." Mack explained the situation.

"For someone back home so short a time, Mack," Dale said, "you sure have worked yourself into one hell of a mess."

"I guess."

"Does that mean Wanda's available?"

"As available as she wants to be."

"Good. She's a real nice person."

"Treat her like one then," Ben said with enough force to surprise Dale.

"Yes, sir, Ben! I guess I better get going. It's been one hell of a day. First, that girl was murdered, now this."

"You got any idea," Roy asked, "who murdered the girl?"

"None yet. We verified who she was with. It was Jason and the dead girl's friend. She never made it to the house when they dropped her off. So far, there doesn't seem to be any obvious motive for the killing. It wasn't rape or robbery, that we've also verified. She was whacked on the back of the head with something, like a piece of pipe or a tire iron, by someone pretty strong. The medical examiner said she died almost instantly, and she was only hit once."

"Jason again," Roy said. "Are you sure he didn't do it?"

"I only know he's got an alibi."

"Too bad. I'd feel a lot better if he was locked up." Roy went on to tell Dale about the incident Mack had with the mugger. He finished with "And Mack didn't give it another thought until he heard about the murdered girl and learned what the murder weapon might be."

"I definitely agree with all of you and your concern for Mack and Mandy. It'd be a real good idea if they're very careful until all of this is resolved."

The phone rang. Ben answered it. The call was for Dale.

"Oh, no," he said after taking the call, "I'll be right in." He hung up the phone. "The sheriff just blew his brains out."

"Been a hell of a night," Ben said, "I hope this is near the end of it."

"Somehow," Roy said, "my gut says it ain't."

Chapter 32

Jason woke up in a foul mood. His head pounded from two nights of heavy drinking and little sleep. He was angry because Mandy hadn't returned as he expected her to and because Elaine hurried home directly from work to be with her husband.

He showered and shaved as he normally did, then left home without making breakfast. What was the sense in eating at home when he was forced to cook it himself?

The first person Jason saw when he arrived at the bank, after eating his breakfast at Katie's Kafe, stopped him.

"Did you hear about the sheriff?" he was asked. "Who'd have thought?"

"I didn't hear anything. I just got here." He hadn't heard anything at Katie's because no one there ever talked to him. The waitresses hated him for his lack of tips and nearly all the other customers worked for a living. "What did the sheriff do?"

"Killed himself. Blew his brains out."

"Do you know why he did it? Did he leave a note?"

"I don't know. I think it's weird."

"I guess it is," Jason said, his hangover helping him keep his voice flat and sounding unconcerned.

Jason was worried. What if the sheriff left a note exposing all of them? Was it time to cut his losses and run? Or would it be better to sit back and wait? If there was no note, he was sure he was safe. None of the stumblebum cops in this county were likely to figure out how involved he was. Either way, he'd begin liquidating most of the investments he made for the sheriff. He'd set up new accounts, using a phony social security number, and get the money moving around. If he moved the money fast enough, using new accounts and social security numbers each time, it'd be virtually impossible to trace. Even the sheriff's wife didn't know about most of the investments. It was unlikely anyone did, considering where the money came from.

Condolences were in order. Maybe he should pay the grieving widow a visit this afternoon, show her his compassion and sorrow. He'd represent the bank too, and offer to help her get the sheriff's estate in order. Wouldn't want her going without everything she had coming. Except, of course, the money that was never really hers. It was all his now. It'd more than double his own investments in Lands Magnificent stock, which were considerable. The sheriff's money made his own losses insignificant, even though he'd have more of them if Ben Thomas's auction was not stopped. The auction was something else he'd better check out, now that the sheriff was dead. Jason called Elaine first.

"You hear about it?" he asked her.

Elaine told him what she knew about the sheriff and the fire, finishing with "And there was little or no damage done to the buildings. I don't know anything else and I have to go. Rich is bowling Friday night. See you then. At the usual spot and time. Bye."

Jason was unable to concentrate on his work and, in a short time, knew he wouldn't accomplish anything until he learned more. He called the sheriff's office.

"This is Jason Cheman," he told the person answering the phone. "I just heard the terrible news about the sheriff. He and his dear wife Teresa were good friends. Is there any indication as to why he did it?"

"Any indication one way or the other, Jason, is and will be for some time, official police business. So I can't comment."

"Let me talk to whoever is in charge."

"You're talking to him."

"Who the hell are you? Don't you know who I am?"

"This is Dale Magee, Jason, and I know exactly who you are. You'll wait until our investigation is over before I give you any information, the same as everyone else."

"Look, Dale, we went to school together. I'm going to see Teresa today. I'd appreciate it if you could tell me enough to give her a little comfort."

"It's a bad situation. You'll still have to wait."

Jason hung up, wondering what Dale meant about a bad situation. It was time to go see the widow. Find out what she knew. It'd be pleasant holding her pretty little hands anyway. One never knew what grief could lead to if she was alone. Jason believed he knew women well enough to detect a certain look.

With luck, he could take advantage of it.

Chapter 33

Roy had trouble sleeping, so he was up before anyone else. After a cup of coffee, he went outside. A reporter from the local radio station came a short time later. Roy told him what happened during the night and a little about the upcoming auction. The reporter left, and less than an hour later, the story was the feature on the station's newscast. They covered the fire and the deaths of the drug dealers, then talked at length about the auction and the incredible number of antiques and collectibles that were going to be sold.

Roy didn't think much about it and only mentioned it in passing to Mack and Ben over breakfast. Mandy and Wanda heard the newscast, and they were full of questions when they got there.

When their questions were answered and the previous night's events were thoroughly discussed, they went to work. While Mandy and Wanda washed and sorted, Mack and Roy carried the last of what was in the attic down to them. Ben went outside. By noon, the attic was empty. It was raining again, so Mack continued to work with Mandy and Wanda. Roy decided he'd rather be wet than in the house.

"You'll only be in the way in here anyway," Mandy told him.

A van from one of the Twin Cities television stations drove in on their way to the barn. Roy answered most of their questions about the night's events. His answers got the reporter curious about the auction, and because she was in love with antiques and a collector of them, they spent more time talking about what was going to be sold at the auction than the shooting. They took a lot of video of the loaded wagons and the barn filled with the various antiques and collectibles. It would give the news department of the station something to fill television screens with while they told the story of the attempted arson and the subsequent deaths of the two men.

Inside the house, Mack was enjoying the time he was spending working with the two women. Mandy took charge, coordinating the work, giving work direction when it was necessary, yet always ready to do any task if Mack and Wanda were busy.

Late in the afternoon, they finished the small items and started on the furniture brought down from the attic. Most of it was in excellent shape and needed nothing more than cleaning. Only minor repairs were attempted on the rest, regluing a table leg or chair rung, nailing together a dresser drawer, or rehanging doors on an old wardrobe. Any major damage was left as it was. They even left the ancient white oak roll-top desk stuck open, knowing it would bring a great price as it was.

By evening, they were finished with the attic. There wasn't much more to do until early morning of the auction, three days away. Ben and Roy were almost finished in the sheds and barn, so it was time to relax. Ben took out a round of beer, with glasses for the ladies, and they sat down at the kitchen table.

"I got to thank you two," Ben said to Mandy and Wanda. "I can't say we'd of done it without you. As it is, all Roy and I got to do for the next couple of days is putz and fuss."

"What about the household things?" Mack asked. "Shouldn't we get all of it ready too, just in case."

"Nope. The auctioneer said when he was here today, there isn't any way there's going to be a need. There's too much to sell as it is."

Mandy smiled. "That's great news, Ben. I'm really happy things are turning out this way."

"Me too. So what're you two gals doing tomorrow?"

"I'm sleeping late," Wanda said. "Then I'm going to clean my apartment, wash clothes, and come out here and drink some beer with you guys."

"How about you, Mandy?"

"Go to the cities. A friend at work gave me the name of a good divorce lawyer. I think it's time I talk to him."

"Good news, Mack?" Roy teased, watching the smile grow on his face. No one noticed the struggle Wanda was having as she tried to keep one on hers.

"Are you two ladies going to be available to help out Sunday? I'll pay you for it, along with the work you already did. I know you'll be more help than the idiots the auctioneer is likely to bring with him."

"We'll be here, Ben," Wanda said, "so long as you don't continue to insult us with talk about money."

"That's right, Ben," Mandy agreed. "Don't bring it up again."

"Damned stubborn women," he said, smiling.

A car drove up to the house. Roy got up and let Dale in.

"What brings you here," Ben asked him, "more trouble?"

"Well, I," Dale stammered, looking at Wanda, "I, uh, stopped to see if Wanda might want to go have a drink with me."

"Now there is an offer too good to refuse." She looked at Mandy. "You guys want to come along?"

"Yeah," Dale said, "why don't you? I'd really like it if you came."

"Sure," Mandy said. "Okay, Mack?"

"Fine by me."

"If you go," Roy said, looking at Mack, "you and Mandy ride with Dale. You all stay together for the night. And watch your backs."

"Oh, Roy," Mandy said, "nothing's going to happen."

Roy looked at Ben a second, sighed, then turned back to Mandy.

"Sorry, Mandy," he said. "I killed two men last night because of that son of a bitch Jason. I don't want to have to kill any more."

"You're right," Mandy said, "I just forgot for a minute. We'll watch our backs."

"Only until they're all locked up," Dale said. "It might be a while before there's enough proof, but it'll happen."

"I hope it's not too long," Mack said.

They went to The Curve because it was a quiet place to sit and talk. They spent a couple of pleasant hours over hamburgers and beer, and then Wanda surprised them.

"I think it's time to go," she said. "I'm going over to Dale's with him for a while. Mandy, do you want to go back to the farm, then take my car back to the apartment, or should we drop both of you off at the apartment now? Dale can take Mack home later, and I can pick up the car then."

"Drop us at the apartment," Mack said.

Mandy and Dale smiled at his answer. Wanda studied her lap.

Chapter 34

Friday started with a steady light rain that lasted all day. Ben and Roy contented themselves in the barn, sorting and rearranging boxes, trays, and furniture to make it easier for auction day. A constant stream of visitors stopped to check out the things to be sold at the auction. They didn't think much about it at first, until they talked to several of them and realized how many were from other areas in the state, especially the Twin Cities. There were even a few from Iowa and Wisconsin. They realized then that the television station they talked to had featured the video of the auction merchandise when they covered the attempted arson on their six and ten o'clock news casts. Other stations picked up the story and featured it on their morning news shows. Jason's fire had given them more free advertising than they could have imagined. Mack was unaware of what was going on because he had decided it would be a good time to pay Rich a visit at the refuge. Elaine was alone in the refuge office when he got there.

"He's working out in the field," she answered curtly when he asked about Rich.

"Is it the same thing he was working on before?" Mack asked, knowing that if it was, it would be easy to find him.

"Yeah, I guess. I'll tell him you were here."

Mack left without attempting further conversation. He went out to the refuge. Rich's truck was parked in the same place Mack found it on his previous visit. Mack slipped on his rain gear, then found Rich near the river, sitting quietly on a tree stump.

"I think I'll get me a government job," Mack teased as he walked up behind him. "Won't need to work anymore then."

Rich turned around. "You bet, Mack. It'll be a good time for you to learn how to put up with more bullshit than you ever imagined."

"I thought you spent more time with the critters than the crap."

"Used to. Not the last couple of years, though."

"What changed?"

"Why do you always ask me questions I'd be better off not answering?"

"An incessant curiosity. And this time, a need to know."

"What do you need to know this time?"

"All about the project and how it's going to affect this refuge."

"I expect you know too much already."

"Too many things are happening. People are getting killed because of it. The refuge is going to be royally screwed up by it."

"What makes you say that? According to the environmental impact study we're working on, the refuge will benefit in the long run."

"Who's doing the study, Rich?"

"Does it matter?"

"You bet it matters. A blind man can see that if you dam the river to flood it here, it's going to back up into the flats north of here. How the hell are you going to control water levels with the control gates under water?"

"Won't have to. Be more water available."

"Deep water, sure. Won't do anything for shallow feeding ducks, will it? It'll screw up the natural cycles of wet and dry too. You're the one who taught me how it all works and the reasons for the controls. So you know it won't be better. Most of the refuge won't work the way it should. How much wildlife will be lost?"

"Half, maybe more. But fishing will be better, Mack."

"Are you going to open more of it for fishing? Ray was always against it. He said that old fishing lines and those plastic deals that hold six packs of beer together kill more ducks than hunters do."

"Ray's dead."

"I think maybe that's why."

"You think he shot himself because he was depressed about the ducks?"

"I think he was murdered."

"The sheriff doesn't."

"The sheriff's dead too."

"I know, Mack. For the first time in my life, I know what's going on around me. It's taught me a lot. Now I don't know if I can keep doing it. If I stay here, I'll spend most of my time babysitting jerks that should be kept out. Maybe I'll take my wife's advice and accept the office job I was offered."

"I'd hate to see you do that. You're one of those rare people I've known who really care about the environment."

"What good does it do? If people actually cared about it, Mack, there wouldn't be any project."

"I still don't think you should quit. Why does your wife want you to take an office job? I thought she wanted to stay here. Didn't she grow up in this area?"

"I forgot, you've been gone a long time." Rich smiled sadly. "My wife died a few years back. Cancer. Got a new one now."

"Really! Anyone I'd know?"

"You met her in the office. Elaine."

"Good-looking woman."

"That she is." Rich sighed heavily, shaking his head. "But you'd think at my age, I'd have enough sense to keep the pecker harnessed."

"Why would you want to, married to a looker like her?"

"There's more to life than looks. I think she means well," Rich said, more because he thought he should than because he believed it, "even if she is a lot more ambitious than I am. She says she wants me to go back to Washington with her."

"Is that where she came from? The Northwest is beautiful, so it's hard to fault her for wanting to go back."

"She wants to go back to Washington, DC, Mack. She worked there before she was transferred out here to assist us with our environmental impact studies. They want to make sure that those of us in the field do things right."

"That's kind of strange, isn't it? I thought it was your job. You, Ray, Jerry, all of you guys who work here."

"It was until we didn't do it right."

"How didn't you do it right? You tell the truth too often?"

"I think we've talked enough, Mack."

"I think we just started, Rich. There must be some way to stop it."

"Nothing less than the people in this area caring about more than their wallets will do it. That, and teaching some men to cool their ambition to be the boss and others to keep it in their pants."

"You referring to you and Jerry?"

"Take it how you like it. You and I both wonder about Ray. He never backed down from the fight against the project. Never gave in to the powers that be."

Rich stood, picked up a rock, and threw it hard into the river. "See you around, Mack. It's time you got the hell out of here. Oh, and tell your dad I wish him the best of luck Sunday."

"Thanks, Rich. Maybe we can talk again sometime?"

"Maybe. You never can tell what might happen."

Mack was feeling down when he got home. If men like Jerry and Rich, who at one time dedicated their lives to preserving the environment, could sell out for so little, how would any of it be saved? It was a silly question and he knew it. None of it would. Rich was right. Whatever it was he did, it would never make any difference unless ordinary people started to care enough to make some sacrifices. He continued to brood about it until Wanda stopped by late in the afternoon. She was quiet at first, embarrassed about the night before. He sat her down at the table with a couple of beers.

"It's okay that you like Dale. You don't have to slink around here like you did something wrong."

"I think I might have. To do what I did, I should feel more for him than I do."

"It looked to me as though you liked him."

"I do. I like him a lot. It's just…"

"It's okay. Don't make a big deal out of it."

She sighed. "So when's Mandy going to get back from the lawyer's?"

"Soon, I hope. I'm kind of worried with her going all the way to the cities alone."

"She went to Minnetonka, didn't she? I heard that it's one of the nicest suburbs."

"It's not Minnetonka I'm worried about."

"Yeah, Jason. You're going to have to get used to it, Mack. Next week, she'll be back at work. She'll be going down there every day. You can't spend every minute worrying about her. You'll go crazy."

"It's hard not to worry. So are you going out with Dale again tonight?"

"I don't know that we're going out. He's meeting me here."

"Mandy's coming right here too. Would you like to do something with us again?"

"Yes, I'd like that very much, Mack."

"Good. Stop looking so down. You look the same as I've felt all day."

"Why do you feel down?"

Mack told her about his visit with Rich.

"Do you really believe no one cares about the refuge or the environment?"

"It's not only that they don't care, they also don't understand. Economic benefit, no matter how short term, is always important to everyone. So nothing's going to change."

"I think you're exaggerating, Mack. Things aren't so bad."

"That's my point exactly. Good jobs, kissing ass, and putting up with the lies of the rich and powerful. That's what's important, what matters."

"When you believe in something, Mack, you sure don't back off or give in a bit. You're almost as stubborn as your dad and Roy. And more sarcastic."

"I hope so. Ready for another beer?"

As Mack got up to get the beers, Mandy drove in the yard, so he took out three, gave one to Wanda, and handed one to Mandy as soon as she came inside.

"Thanks," Mandy said. "It's been a long day."

"Problems with the lawyer?"

"No, it's just frustrating, trying to figure out what Jason's been doing with all the money. We'll both be spending a lot of time working on it."

"At least," Wanda said, "you'll have more time to do it."

Chapter 35

Rich had some time left after he got ready to go bowling, so he waited around, watching Elaine get dressed. As always, he reacted as she covered her ample breasts with a sheer bra, lifting them slightly without hiding them. She smiled, knowing he was watching, knowing what she did to him and that was why she could control him.

"I thought you were going bowling."

"I've got a while yet. I like watching you dress. Turns me on."

"You waited too long. You should've asked me before I got dressed."

"I'm not asking."

"You have that gleam in your eye."

"I usually do when I look at you. It can wait until I get home tonight."

"Good, it'll be better then."

Damn, she thought, *now I'll have to hurry home in time to shower before he gets here. I won't be able to have as much time with Jason. I'll be glad when I can get rid of this jerk.*

She looked at Rich again, knowing she had a way to finish him for the night. She joined him on the bed, running her hands over him, then unzipping him.

"I'll give you a little of my magic," she said, pulling him loose, "to hold you until later."

Rich knew what she was doing and hated himself for letting her do it. Much too soon, he groaned. She held him a moment, then emptied her mouth into a folded tissue.

"That should satisfy you for a while," she said, getting up and going into the bathroom. Rich waited until she came out before he left the house.

"I'll take the van back to the maintenance area," she said, "before I go into town."

"Good enough," he agreed, "I'll see you when I get home."

Rich hadn't told Elaine his bowling was canceled. He drove directly to the maintenance area, backed his truck among some trees not far from her car, and waited. He wanted to find out who she was seeing tonight. He'd known for a long time that she was involved with someone. She had to be. She was gone too often, and her excuses were too flimsy. He'd proved it the last time he followed her to a meeting with Jason and the sheriff. There was only one explanation for her short visit with the sheriff in the back of the van.

An hour went by. Why did she say she was bringing the van back if she wasn't going to? Why would she want to drive that big ugly rig instead of her car, a bright red sporty model, with an engine too big for its size? She loved cruising around in it, showing off her driving skills. He knew he was asking questions he had the answer for. Next time, he'd follow her from home.

Rich left the maintenance area. He drove south on roads bordering the west side of the refuge. As was his habit, he slowed as he passed each gate, checking to be sure they were closed and locked. It wasn't uncommon for teenagers, and sometimes adults, to break a lock or use a volunteer's key to get in. It was a good place for parties and for sex.

Along the south leg, where the road didn't border the refuge, an old township road ran east as far as the refuge border. The road had served a few ragged houses and mobile homes until they were bought up by the project people. A light rain was falling, softening the road's surface, so the tracks someone had recently made were easy to see.

He didn't go in the gate. What was the point? It was probably kids parked inside, having a good time. This part of the refuge would soon be gone, so what harm could they do? Besides, he'd sold his soul for the same thing. He drove to town and stopped at the local VFW post. The bar area was nearly empty, with only a small group at a table, and a pretty but tired-looking lady sitting alone at the bar. He sat down next to her.

"Hi," he said. "My name is Rich and I could use some company for a while. Mind if I sit here?"

"No, Rich, I don't mind. My name is Teresa. My husband shot himself a couple of days ago, and I don't know how to be alone tonight."

She smiled and looked into his eyes. Hers were large and green and filled with a strange sparkle. He knew he should go home but didn't.

Chapter 36

The familiar sounds and smells of Ben working in the kitchen woke Mack. First, it was a muffled clang from Ben setting the heavy cast-iron frying pan on the stove to heat. Then the rattle of the old porcelain coffeepot as he got it ready. The smells of perking coffee and frying bacon followed.

Mack got out of bed, walked to the window, and looked outside. Stars were shining bright in the light of the pale new moon. He opened the window, drinking the fresh, clean air, relishing the warm breeze. The room quickly filled with the scent of deep summer, blending pleasantly with the cooking odors coming up from the kitchen.

He drew in the deepest breath he could. As far as he was concerned, there was nothing like it. Not the new life of a fresh spring day nor the brilliant colors of a crisp autumn morning could match a late summer day when the natural life around them had reached maturity. He dressed and went downstairs. Ben poured him a mug of coffee as he sat down at the table.

"Never thought I'd see you up this early, Mack," Ben said. "It's only three. Figured you to sleep until sunup."

"The boy's growing up," Roy said.

Mack smiled, knowing they couldn't let it go by without some kidding. "It's going to be a perfect day," he said. "Must be sixty, sixty-five degrees out there. Probably won't get more than seventy-five today. We couldn't ask for better weather for an auction. We should have a good crowd today."

"I was just hoping that the rain would stop," Ben said. "Now all I've got to do is hope it doesn't start up again."

"Doesn't look like it will," Roy said. "There isn't a cloud in the sky."

"Could change. Wouldn't be nothing new if it did. Not in this part of the world. Don't forget, Roy, this is Minnesota, not Texas."

"It's not going to change," Mack said. "This is going to be a perfect summer day. You're going to have a great auction."

"I hope. What time are the girls coming? The auction starts at ten."

"Actually, they just drove in."

"Be damned. Guess I better throw some more bacon and biscuits on."

Mandy and Wanda came in looking tired, as if they were hours away from being ready for the day. Ben had coffee waiting for them before they sat down.

"How many eggs can you eat?" he asked them.

"Only one," Wanda answered.

"Just coffee for me," Mandy said. "I never eat breakfast."

"The hell you say. We got a mess of work to do today. You got to eat."

"Really, Ben," Mandy pleaded, "I'm not at all hungry."

"You got to eat anyway."

"But…"

"Don't bother to argue, Mandy," Roy told her. "Ben says you got to eat, it's best you do. It'll ruin his day if you don't."

"Okay. One egg."

Ben smiled and turned back to the stove. When he faced them again, it was to serve the food. Mandy and Wanda were each served hash browns topped with two eggs, biscuits, and several thick slices of bacon. Mack and Roy got the same, with double the potatoes and four eggs. Before Ben sat down at the table, a platter of each item was set in the middle of the table to ensure everyone would get enough to eat. Only a few slices of bacon and some biscuits were left when the meal was done.

"Figured you could eat," Ben said to Mandy.

"Knew you could," he told Wanda.

"If I ate like this every day," Mandy complained, "I'd be too fat to walk."

"This isn't any ordinary day, Mandy," Roy said, "and when it's over, you'll be thinner than you were when you got here."

After they finished their coffee, Wanda volunteered for the kitchen cleanup. The rest of them went outside to begin the final preparations for the auction. Ben and Roy went into the barn to carry out the furniture. Mack and Mandy pulled the tarps off the wagons. Nearly all that could be done was done when the first light peeked over the eastern horizon. The rest of the moving and organizing would be done as the auction progressed.

"What an absolutely gorgeous morning," Mandy said as they paused to watch the sunrise. "I wish I could have a million more just like this."

"I don't know if you'll see that many," Ben said, "but at your age, you've got a lot of them ahead of you. You and Mack. You too, Wanda."

The first customer drove in, and Mack directed them to the grassy field they'd designated for parking. As soon as the pickup was in the right spot, he put up signs to direct traffic to the parking area. Before he finished, five more vehicles were parked in the field. By the time the auctioneer arrived, the field was nearly full. Close to a hundred people were lined up for bidding numbers before the auctioneer's people were ready to assign them. Mandy sat down with the auction clerks to help hand them out. Wanda and Mack got another parking area ready that they hadn't thought they'd need. It was full by nine, with people still coming. As they reached auction time, cars and trucks were lined along both sides of the road for three quarters of a mile in both directions. Many of the trucks, in the parking areas and on the road, had the names of antique stores painted on the sides, and enough of the cars were Cadillacs and other high-end vehicles to indicate there was a lot of money in the crowd. Everyone involved was called over to the auctioneer's truck just before it was time to start.

"Here's how I'd like to do it," the auctioneer said. "Ben, you and your boy stick around the barn, tell my guys what goes on the wagons as they fill them. Don't get so fussy you slow things down. We want them filled as quick as we can after we empty them. Give folks a chance to look things over before they bid on it. You, young lady," he pointed at Mandy, "I think can do the most good by keeping the tally. My clerks will sort and total tickets by bidding number as they're brought in. You tally up their totals as we go along. We need to know the numbers before we start any bidding on the property. We want to cancel that if we can, and I think we will. In between, you can run the tickets from the clerk who's in the truck with me writing up the bids to the clerk you're working with. Don't let them pile up. Anyone who wants to settle up and go, we want them out of here. They ain't bidding, they're in the way. Roy, I'd like you and this other pretty young lady to help on the wagons. You know the drill so you tell her what to do. You'll be up there about two hours at a time, then you'll have an hour or two off. Use the toilet now if you need to. Gets embarrassing if you all the sudden got to run off. I know, I did it a couple a times. Any questions?"

They didn't have any.

"Good. Let's make this great crowd happy and start this puppy. We got a hell of a lot of shit to sell today."

"See," Ben said, "I told you it was just junk."

"Ben, you silly ass, when you see the totals tonight, nothing will ever be junk again. Let's do her."

The auctioneer climbed up into the back of the special topper on his pickup. It sat high over the crowd so he could see any hands raised to make a bid and had a public address system built in, with speakers standing on tripods scattered around the yard.

"Okay, folks, it's time to start," the auctioneer began. "First, I want to thank Ben Thomas for asking me to conduct this auction. I believe what we have here today is the finest selection of antiques I've ever seen assembled at one auction, so bid often and bid high. You'll never again get the chance to buy a lot of what we'll be selling today. You need a number to bid, so if you haven't got one, get it now. I won't be waiting on you. Most of you know the terms of the auction.

You buy it and you own it. You're responsible for what you buy, not us. Someone steals it, you pay for it anyway, so watch your stuff. Payment is cash, good check, or plastic, MasterCard or Visa. We're going to handle this one a little different today and sell the higher priced antiques on the wagons first. A lot more than what you see now will be coming out of the barn. We'll be loading wagons as we empty them, so you'll get a chance to see what's there before it's bid on. The furniture will follow, then the machinery. Last, we'll finish up the wagons and whatever else is left. Roy, what are we going to start with?"

Roy picked up a six-pack of seven-ounce Coca-Cola bottles in the original cardboard carton. The bidding was fast, ending at twenty-five dollars. The auctioneer made no attempt to squeeze more out of the crowd and instantly started the bidding on the wood tabletop radio Wanda was holding high in the air so everyone could see it. It went for fifty. Ben, who was watching with his mouth open wide, turned to Mack.

"You see that, Mack?" he asked. "Twenty-five dollars for some goddamn pop bottles that haven't even got any use."

"That's why they're valuable. Looks like there are some collectors here today."

"Collectors? People collect old pop bottles?"

"Especially Coke. Most people who collect Coca-Cola things collect anything that has to do with it. Pay attention today. Maybe you'll learn a few things."

"Now don't be a smart-ass," Ben grumbled, turning back to the bidding.

The auctioneer kept the bidding moving at a steady pace, just fast enough to keep the bidders on edge, only occasionally cracking a joke or commenting on the item bid on. Without interfering, Roy kept a constant commentary going on about what was sold and who bought it. Wanda picked up on what Roy was doing and started answering most of his comments. Soon, they were making cracks about each other, then flirting. They kept the crowd in a lighthearted mood and the bidding grew heavier, the prices growing ever higher, often more than the value of the item sold.

The auction continued at a fast pace, so Mack and Ben were kept busy giving work direction to the auctioneer's crew, loading wagons, and answering questions from people in the crowd who wanted to know about specific items coming up for bid. It wasn't far into the auction that it turned into a fuzzy blur floating somewhere over their heads. The constant chant of the auctioneer, mixed in with the crowd noise, became a single deafening sound that neither Mack nor Ben heard any longer. Suddenly, it was quiet.

"Please, everyone, I have an announcement to make," the auctioneer said.

Mack stopped to listen. Ben joined him, his hand resting on Mack's shoulder. Mandy was on the truck, holding a sheet of paper in front of the auctioneer.

"I can't tell you how pleased I am to say this. As you know, we originally planned to sell the real estate at about noon. It ain't gonna happen, folks. You've been kind enough to bid fairly and often enough, so the real estate is not going to be sold. Not today and not until Ben Thomas chooses to sell it. He's got no need to now."

A cheer went up in the crowd. As loud from the people there who never knew Ben, as it was from those who did know him. There weren't many people in the crowd who didn't watch the news on television.

Mack felt a big hand squeeze his shoulder. When he turned to look at Ben, he pretended not to notice the tears welling in his father's eyes.

The auctioneer quieted the crowd after a couple of minutes. "Okay, folks, we gotta get back to it. There's still a hell of a lot left to sell. Roy, what have you got?"

"Wait a minute," someone in the crowd yelled. "You just wait a damn minute. You have to sell the real estate. It was advertised."

Jason pushed his way through the crowd.

"All the auction bills and ads," the auctioneer told him, "clearly state that everything is subject to change the day of the sale. There's nothing new to that, Jason, and you know damn well there isn't."

"I'll have your license for this," Jason threatened.

The auctioneer rolled his eyes, then turned to Roy. "Would you look at what the man has there, folks? That chest is full of carpenter's tools. Each and every one a genuine antique. It's a complete matched set. I'm going to start the bid on the whole unit. You've got to want it, folks. If I don't like the final bid, I'll break it up and sell it piece by piece. What's the first bid, do I hear a thousand?"

To even his surprise, he got an immediate bid at a thousand. The bidding stopped at ten thousand, five hundred. Jason waited for the end of the bid, glared up at Mandy, who was still in the auctioneer's truck, shook his fist, and walked away, disappearing in the crowd.

"What an asshole," Mandy said on her way out of the truck, loud enough for the PA system to pick it up. Her remark got the biggest laugh of the day.

The crowd thinned as the day wore on. The bidding continued on the high side anyway. Late in the afternoon, Mack's old saddle came up for bid. The auctioneer asked for an opening bid of twenty-five dollars.

"Two hundred," Roy bid instantly. "I drove up here from Texas," he told the crowd, "to buy this saddle. So I damn well plan to own it."

Two hundred dollars was slightly more than the saddle was worth, but suddenly several people in the crowd were sure, because Roy started the bid so high, that it must be worth more. Before the bidding was over, the saddle cost Roy five hundred. He tried to buy the blacksmith's tools too. He quit at a thousand. They sold for more than double that.

At 6 p.m., the auctioneer stopped again.

"Okay, folks," he said, "we've still got a lot left to sell. Way I look at it, we've got two choices. Keep going until every last thing is sold or quit now and finish it off next Sunday. It's up to you. If we're going to continue, though, I need to know enough of you will stay around to the end of it."

An overwhelming portion of the crowd wanted to continue, so they did. As the evening wore on and the prices dropped, the bidding moved faster. A lot of what really was junk was sold in lots, several boxes or piles sold in one bid, rather than bidding on each item. They finished after ten, in the dark. It took another hour to get everyone settled up with the clerks and two more after that to total the money taken in.

Ben invited everyone connected to the auction into the house while they waited. Beer was passed around to those who wanted any and pop to the rest. Because they had to work the next day, Mandy and Wanda quit after one beer, then told Ben they were leaving. He gave each of them a huge hug and kiss on the cheek before he'd let them out the door.

"I've got to tell you," he said, "I'd be more than proud to have either one of you as my daughter. This never would've gotten done if you two weren't here to make sure we did it right. I owe the both of you."

"We're just happy, Ben," Wanda said, "that we could help."

Mandy kissed his cheek, her tears flowing too heavily to say anything. He made it clear she was accepted, and it was all she wanted. They were all tired, so there wasn't much talk while they waited for the final numbers. Mack was the only one who felt a restless energy, a feeling of something left undone, but he wasn't sure what was bothering him. When the auctioneer brought the check for the auction proceeds over to Ben, however, and waved him and Roy over to see it, Mack's mood changed.

"Wow, yes, great" was all he managed to say.

Roy simply smiled and nodded. Ben didn't say or do anything. He just stood there staring at the check.

"What do you think about junk now, Ben?" asked the auctioneer.

"Don't know that I'll ever use the word again. Think I might choke on it if I did."

Chapter 37

Ben was up an hour before dawn, the same as he was every morning. Roy followed when breakfast was started. They let Mack sleep. After breakfast, Ben showered and got ready to go to town, anxious to get to the bank to deposit the auction check and pay off the note on the farm. He returned to the kitchen wearing his best suit, normally worn only to weddings and funerals, a white shirt, tie, and polished shoes.

"What the hell is the get-up for?" Roy asked him.

"Figured I ought to look decent if we're going to talk to the bankers today."

"You go dressed the way you are, Ben, you're showing them respect. That's the last thing either one of us should do today. Go put on your work clothes and make sure they need washing. We're going to do some real thumb nosing today, and if we stink some doing it, so much the better."

"You know, Roy," Ben said, grinning, "you got more ways of kicking ass and getting even than any man I ever knew."

"It improves life when you learn how."

Ben changed and, this time, came out wearing the same pair of overalls he wore the last two days before the auction. The collar on his shirt was ragged, his boots were worn and scuffed, and he had a red plaid handkerchief hanging out of his back pocket, just for show.

"This better?"

"It is," Roy said. "You're now a dumb farmer and I'm a stupid cowboy." He pushed himself into an artificial pose, showing off his faded jeans, frayed western shirt, and high-heeled cowboy boots.

"Now find yourself one of those caps, with John Deere or some such thing on it, and we're ready to go. I already got my cowboy hat ready."

"Who's driving?" Ben asked as they left the house.

"Me. You'll be coming home in your new truck, and I'm not about to drive that old heap of yours."

"Hey now, she's done me fine for a lot of years."

"You ought to junk it now."

"Can't. Wouldn't be fair to her. Make a good field truck anyway."

"If you say so."

When they got to town, they stopped at a relatively new bank, where Ben had never done business. It was located directly across the street from the Kingsburg State Bank where he'd always kept his accounts.

"Can I help you?" asked the gray-haired receptionist.

"You bet," Roy told her, "we need to see the president or whatever you call the head man around here."

"I'm sorry, sir, he's in a meeting. Can someone else help you?"

"Nope. Tell him he can un-meet himself. Ben Thomas wants to see him right now."

"I'm not allowed…"

"Today you are, ma'am. If you ain't smart enough to find him, we'll be doing it ourselves."

She picked up the phone, and within one minute, the bank president was out greeting them, then showing them the way to his office.

"That was quite an auction you had yesterday, Mr. Thomas. What I can do for you today?"

"It's like this," Roy said when they were seated, "I'm acting as Ben's agent for a while." He nodded to Ben and Ben handed the banker the auction check. "What you got to do is tuck this thing away for Ben in such a way that it's safe and insured and all that. About thirty thousand goes into a checking account, the rest into savings of some kind. It's gotta be something solid. You also got to call the assholes across the street, find out the balance on the note Ben's got on his place, then issue a cashier's check for the amount, so we can go over there and pay it off while we close his accounts. You will immediately cover any and all checks Ben might want to write today. None of this crap about how you got to wait for his deposit check to clear. You know who wrote it, and you know it's good. Can you do that in the next ten, fifteen minutes?"

"Yes, sir, no problem." He picked up the phone, mumbled into it, turned red and said, "Damn it, do it!" and hung up. "We'll have everything ready for you as fast as humanly possible."

"Good," Roy said, "'cause we ain't in the waiting mood today. Ben's buying hisself a new truck, and we're kind of anxious to get out there and deal."

"We'll finance it," the banker said, "if you want us to."

"No way," Ben said. "I'm out from under now and I plan to stay that way."

"Tell me if you would, Mr. Thomas, are you planning to sell your farm?"

"Why do you ask?"

"We'd like to buy it."

"I don't think," Roy said, "you want to pay Ben what he wants for it now."

Roy told him the price.

"That's four times its market value."

"Not if that big project is going to be built the way it's supposed to be built. If it's going to, they're paying good money to do it. You've got until our business here is finished to write Ben a check for the amount I quoted you, then the price goes up."

"It's too steep for us."

"That's fine. Probably too steep for them people over to the other bank too. Make Ben's boy Mack happier than hell to keep the refuge what it is, anyhow. Ain't none of us need no damn resort."

"You know, if you stop the project, a lot of people around here will be hurt."

"Only those so filled with greed they deserve to be."

Within thirty minutes, Ben and Roy were inside the Kingsburg State Bank, waiting for a teller to close out Ben's accounts.

"Amazing, isn't it," Roy said to Ben as they waited, "how loud money talks to a banker?"

"It looks like it, Roy. I wonder, ain't we pushing this a little too hard?"

"Nope, might not be hard enough. You're way too easy on these people."

The teller returned.

"I'm sorry," she said. "Mr. Cheman wants to see you before I close any of your accounts."

"Excuse my real bad language here, ma'am," Roy said, "but tell Jason to go fuck himself. Then send the top headman, who is the boss of this outfit, out here to talk to us. We ain't going nowhere!"

The teller disappeared, then quickly returned with a plump red-faced man.

He forced a smile and stuck his hand out to Ben. "I'm Gary Brown, the president of the bank, Mr. Thomas," he said. "Would you mind stepping into our meeting room so we can discuss this?"

Ben stood quietly, looking at the man's hand as if he'd just pulled it out of an overflowing cesspool.

"We'll talk," Roy said, "after you get done what we came in here to do. So get your fat ass together and do it. Now!"

"But…"

"Come on, Ben," Roy said, bluffing, "let's go see that lawyer fella we was talking to earlier."

The man nodded at the teller, who quickly went back into her cage. "It's being done. Will you please give us a few moments of your time while you wait? I would very much appreciate it."

"That's all you're going to get," Roy answered.

They followed him into the bank's meeting room. Seated at the big table were Jason; Rodney Twilabee, the CEO of Lands Magnificent Corporation; and Susan Spenser, the secretary. Gary Brown sat down and motioned for Ben and Roy to do so.

"We'll stand," Roy said, "so hurry up and say what you got to say. We've been here long enough already."

"Please," said Twilabee, "sit down."

"Who the hell are you?" Roy asked.

"The name is Rodney Twilabee. I am the chief executive officer of Lands Magnificent Corporation."

"So?"

"We own this bank."

"So?"

"So we want to buy Mister Thomas's farm and are prepared to make a very generous offer. Please sit down so we can discuss it."

"Make your offer," Roy said without moving.

"Who are you?" Twilabee asked.

"Ben's acting agent."

"Can you please give me your name?"

"It's Roy." Jason chimed in. "He's Ben's brother."

"We're both Mr. Thomas to you, wimp," Roy shot back. He turned to Twilabee. "If you want to talk at all, you'll be smart enough to tell that small piece of nothing sitting over there to keep his mouth shut."

"Jason!" Twilabee said, barely glancing in his direction. "Okay, Roy, will you sit down now?"

"Mr. Thomas, and no, we won't sit down, so get to it. What's the offer?"

"We are offering your brother, Mr. Thomas, one hundred and fifty thousand dollars for his farm."

Roy laughed, short and hard. "You ain't even close." He told them in detail, while using short sentences, everything they were asking for.

"That's outrageous," Jason said.

"Not hardly," Roy said, "but since Jason here thinks it is, the price just went up another fifty thousand."

"You know we can't pay you such an outrageous sum, Mr. Thomas," Twilabee said. "Please be reasonable."

Roy looked at Ben. "You're keeping total, Ben. Add another twenty-five thousand to the price of your farm." Roy turned back to Twilabee. "None of you jackasses thought it was an unreasonable thing to do when you sprayed Ben's crops with poison so you could run him off his land. You ain't thought about a damn thing. You tried to burn him out, you went gunning for him and his boy Mack, and I believe Jason here was in on the murder of the manager over at the refuge. So you can all go to hell. You should of thought of what you're getting from us now before you did to us what you did. We're leaving now. Before we go, I've got to tell you that you'd best check into the smell of a real big hog feeding operation. Think about what it'll do for your fancy resort. Particularly when someone as conscientious as Ben here spreads the pig shit on his fields on a daily basis. The price for the farm won't go down, only up. You decide to make a deal, you bring a proposal out to Ben's place. Written in plain English, with no fine print or lawyer garbage, and then we'll talk about it. The deal won't be done no other way."

They left the meeting room, settled the business with the bank teller, then left the bank.

"I don't believe I ever heard you talk so much, Roy," Ben said, "unless it was to me."

"No, and I wouldn't of done it, either, if it wasn't so much fun watching them squirm. Jason would've liked to have killed us."

"That he would. It's a little late to do him any good now, though."

"Hope he knows that, Ben."

"I think he does."

"Probably. Let's skip looking for a truck for you today. I think those Landswhatever folks are going to buy it for you. They're getting off too cheap otherwise."

Ben smiled at Roy's comment, knowing that if their demands were met, he'd be rich beyond his wildest dreams.

Chapter 38

"Well, Jason," Twilabee said after Ben and Roy left, "what do you suggest now?"

"We could try to wait him out. A lot of things can go wrong with a hog operation."

"That's pretty limited thinking, Jason. The money it'll cost to wait amounts to a great deal more than what we'll save by waiting. We've just had that proven to us. Besides, I don't think we want to go into the hog poisoning business. Gary, do you have any ideas?"

"I think we should go for the deal. If you think of it from the right angle, Roy's ideas are not so bad nor are they that expensive. Particularly if you take in the publicity aspect."

"How's that?"

"Ben Thomas is an organic farmer. Rather than merely giving him the right to supply the various restaurants and bars with organic produce, we can use his farm as a teaching tool on how to care for the land. Be great publicity for us. Show we're concerned about the environment. That we have a heart. It should help some to combat all the negative crap that was on television a few days ago."

"Good idea. His farm is real old too, isn't it?"

"Over a hundred years," Jason said, struggling now for a way out of the mess he was in. "We could fix up the place, restore the house and barn, maybe turn it into one of the historic wonders of the area, and let people take tours. If we do it right, we can even charge admission."

"Sure," Twilabee agreed, "and replicate other old buildings similar to what were once in the area, for the various fast food and souvenir stands. Maybe turn the whole project into kind of a theme park. Wouldn't take that much. Some false fronts, add horseback riding, a place to pitch horseshoes, maybe a petting zoo for the kiddies, things like that. Maybe call the place Heritage Preservation Minnesota. Give people the feeling we're preserving their history, as well as the land. It's better than having them believe we're destroying their refuge. Making them feel good about what we're doing will also improve the time-share sales of the condos and townhouses. Doing it this way, I think we'll grow faster and farther than we originally planned."

"You go that far," Gary Brown asked, "and where will Ben Thomas live?"

"Buy him a place in town," Jason said. "Or a house not too far away."

"I have a better idea," Twilabee said. "Let's give him a condo… no…one of the townhouses on the lake. A boat too. We'll hire a small crew to help him farm the forty acres he wanted to keep, so he has time to go fishing. Put him on salary, rather than have him selling us the produce. Give the man some security as he gets older. Everyone wants that. If we agree to keep all the land now farmed in vegetable and fruit production, we might convince him to sell all of it, which could save us trouble with his kid down the line. You know, if we handle this right, it might prove to be one hell of a positive move, rather than a negative happening."

"It sounds way too expensive to me," Jason said.

"Jason," Twilabee said, "there's expensive and then there's simply costly. You ought to learn the difference."

"Okay," Jason agreed, "so it's only expensive. How much are you willing to pay Thomas for the property his house is on and the other forty acres? There has to be a limit somewhere."

"We've paid consulting firms more money for fewer ideas than we've gotten today from the farmer and the cowboy. So I think it's time you stopped worrying about nickels and dimes, Jason, and started thinking about getting the job done. You and Susan get with the legal department and write up the proposal. Do it Roy's way. Don't get cute. You do and you're out of here. I expect it on my desk at 8 A.M. tomorrow."

"It'll take all night."

"So be it. You do want to continue your employment here, don't you?"

"Yes, sir," said Jason, his hatred for the Thomas family rapidly growing far beyond what Mack's taking Mandy away from him made him feel.

Chapter 39

Mack was waiting for Ben and Roy when they got home.

"How did it go?" he asked.

"Can't say for certain," Ben answered, "but Roy sure did a fine job on them. They might go for it."

"I believe they will," Roy said. "Can't see where they've got much choice. They sure as hell don't want any hog operation in the middle of their resort."

"You're not going to raise hogs, are you, Dad?"

"No, of course not."

"There's no way," Roy said, "for them to know that. Which means they don't really have much choice."

"Unless they try to burn us out again."

"It wouldn't do them any good, Mack. Ben still owns the land and has insurance to cover the buildings. It only made sense for them to do it before the auction. Insurance never would've covered what was sold."

"I'm beginning to believe Roy's right, Mack. They'll go for the deal. It means there's going to be enough money for better equipment than we ever thought possible. We'll put up a decent-size greenhouse too."

"I think," Roy said, "you two can develop one hell of an operation here. With a ready market for all your produce, you won't be spending your time trying to sell what you grow. That means you can grow more."

"That's right," Ben agreed, "and if there is any excess after we supply their resort, we'll sell it right off the farm to the tourists who stay there. No more getting up at 2 or 3 A.M. to go to the farmer's market."

"It sounds," Mack said, "like a dream come true. But one thing still bothers me."

"What's that, Mack?"

"Shouldn't we be fighting them and trying to save the refuge, rather than giving in to them?"

"How are we going to fight them?" Ben asked. "No one else cares. The refuge isn't the Grand Canyon, and even if it was, I'm not so sure the project could be stopped. Spread enough money around, make promises of a better life, even if they aren't true, and people will go for about anything. If we try to fight them for too long, we'll be taxed out of here, anyway. This way, we've got some control over a small part of what's happening. We'll be able to keep some of the land from being destroyed. I know it isn't much, but I think it's all we've got."

"I don't have to be nice, do I, to the people causing this?"

"No, Mack, you don't. Be best, I think, if you'd try to keep from killing any of them. Even Jason. You got him beat already. You got Mandy."

"I know, I've got her and a hell of a lot more than I ever expected to have. I'd still give it all up to save the refuge."

"Even Mandy."

"I don't believe she's part of this deal, so there's no way I'd ever consider it. The money and an easier life are the parts I'm feeling uncomfortable with."

"It isn't hard to understand how you feel, Mack," Roy said. "It's still better to be staying around and saving what can be saved than walking away and letting it all go. Hang in there, kid. I think you'll end up winning more than you lose."

"I'm not ready to cut and run yet, Roy."

"Good, that's real good, Mack. I hope you never are."

Chapter 40

Mack worried all day about Mandy going back to work and was pacing the floor by the time she got to the farm.

"You scared me," he complained. "You're more than an hour late."

"I know," she said, dropping her head and staring at her shoes, "I'm sorry. I should have called, Mack, just please don't get like Jason and try to put me on a tight schedule so you know what I'm doing every second. I won't live like that again."

"I'm not trying to put you on a schedule, Mandy. I was scared. Right now, I've got too many what-ifs going through my head when you're not where you're supposed to be. Jason is still dangerous."

"I realize that, and I am sorry. The trouble is, there's a lot of work piled on my desk from last week. I still have a job, so you've got to get used to the fact I'll be late sometimes."

"I understand, Mandy. All I'm asking is that you call next time you're running late. It's Jason I don't trust, not you."

"Okay. Plan then that for the rest of this week I'll be working late."

"How long?"

"An hour or so. I think that'll give me enough time to catch up."

"Good. I don't want you out in those parking lots any later. It'd be too easy for something to happen to you with no one around. Someone could easily jump you without being seen, the way they're designed."

"I'll be careful, Mack. So smile and relax, I'm here now."

"I'll try. Is there anything special you want to do tonight?"

"Be with you."

"That's not very specific."

"Maybe not, but Ben and Roy might be listening."

Mack laughed. "How about a walk over to the refuge after supper? There's some really nice spots I'd like to show you before they're gone."

"I can't think of a thing I'd rather do."

Mack packed a blanket and some water in a backpack, and they left right after supper. He led Mandy along some of the trails near the farm until they stopped in a small stand of pines on a ridge overlooking the river. Mandy spread the blanket on the ground while Mack watched the setting sun create magic colors on the water below, wondering how life could have changed so completely, wondering if it could last and somehow afraid it wouldn't.

"Mack, come here."

He turned to see her lying naked on the blanket, smiling and waiting for him. He undressed and joined her, feeling the soft bed of pine needles as he lay down. They made love slowly, letting every sensation, every movement, last and grow. Later, they lay quietly holding each other, knowing they'd belong to each other forever. Both of them believing that no one could ever replace the other.

It was dark as they headed back to the farm. Mack stopped at the edge of the refuge, watching for a moment the outlines of the dark trees, listening to the sounds of the night creatures out feeding.

"It'll be gone soon," he said to her. "It's too bad. I'd like to be able to take you back there again sometime."

"You will. We have lots of time yet."

"The rest of our lives, and there'll be other places. I'll still miss this place when it's gone."

"So will I, Mack."

She took his hand, holding it the rest of the way back to the farm, letting go only when they went inside the house.

Ben and Roy were at their usual spot, sitting at the table with mugs of very black coffee in front of them.

"How's the refuge looking?" Ben asked.

"Sad."

"How's that?"

"It's going to die soon. So it's sad."

"Now, Mack," Mandy argued, "quit brooding about it. We all have too much to be happy about."

"Are you staying tonight, Mandy?" Ben asked.

"No, I'm going back to Wanda's. All my clothes are there."

"I don't know that I like you driving into town alone. I think, considering how bad Jason's been beat up on lately, I'd as soon you move in with us now."

"I don't think I can do that."

"Why not? You're family now. This is where you belong."

"Well, because, you know..."

"It doesn't matter. Not either way. You can have your own room, or you and Mack can take mine. It's the biggest."

"Dad," Mack said, surprised by Ben's offer, "I didn't think you'd ever approve of that."

"Most times and ways I wouldn't, but any fool can see you two made your commitments. That's what really matters. Not some short-term legal technicalities."

"It isn't any of my business," Roy said, "except I have to say this anyway. Ben's right. Best you stay here, Mandy, where it's safe."

"Okay, if you guys care that much, I'll stay. Mack can take me over to Wanda's to get my things."

Mack took her to Wanda's and, after receiving Wanda's blessing on the move, brought her home. Ben and Roy were already in bed. Ben left a note telling them to use his room. Mack had a fire in his belly when he got in bed next to Mandy, not knowing if it was fear or excitement.

He didn't realize it was both.

Chapter 41

Jason hated them all, everyone, and the Thomas family the most. Mack more than anyone. Mack's taking Mandy away from him was one thing, screwing him up at the bank was something he'd never forgive. No one was going to mess with his income and get away with it.

He was working late, probably all night, for the benefit of Ben Thomas, his useless cowboy son Mack, and even for Roy. He'd get all of them. Gary Brown, too, for coming up with the ideas that made things better for Ben and Mack Thomas and worse for himself.

He'd get Twilabee, too, for giving the job of bank president to the likes of Gary Brown. A man who didn't even have any investments, who spent nearly all his income on his wife and kids, then gave the rest to that New World Order Church of his.

Twilabee also added the insult of making him work all night. With no help except the little flea-brained Susan Spenser, who couldn't seem to grasp the value of a dollar. Sure, she could type, whip through research, and use the computer with lightning speed, which she was doing at this very minute, but that wasn't so much. She was merely a woman. Put on earth for the sole purpose of serving him. She hadn't fulfilled her destiny yet. Still wouldn't submit to all of his demands. Wouldn't pay her half of their motel bill. She wasn't meeting his needs. Not as he wanted them filled at this very moment. As he was going to have them filled. The hell with whether or not she was willing. He wanted it, he deserved it, and he was going to have it. If she didn't like it, she could start paying her share of their expenses when they went to a motel.

Jason left his office, found Susan, and filled his hands with her breasts as he stepped behind her. She jumped out of her chair, pushing him away from her.

"Are you nuts? We can't do this here. We'll both get fired if we get caught."

"No one else is around."

"I don't care, Jason. I'm tired already, and we'll probably be working most of the night. Use your energy for that. I'm not a bit in the mood for fooling around right now. So keep your hands off me."

"I can't concentrate. I need it, Susan, so I can stop thinking about it. I think you should get yourself in the mood for me."

"I'm flattered I have that kind of effect on you. I still don't think so. I wouldn't do it here even if I was in the mood. This place turns me off enough as it is. After we get the proposal written, we can go to your place and spend the day in bed if you want to."

"If you really want to marry me, Susan, then you've got to learn to satisfy me when I need you to."

"Don't be silly, Jason. I'm not going to be your slave. God, I don't know what's gotten into you. First you keep trying to do all that weird crap with me. Then you want me to pay for things you can afford and I can't. Now this. I think you better settle down. Go back to work now. We don't have time for this."

"Oh, come on, Susan, I'm not trying to do anything weird. Come here and give me a hug. I'm sorry. I love you."

"Oh, all right."

She moved into his arms. He held her tightly against him and kissed her neck. His hand moved slowly up and down her back while he pushed himself against her, making her feel him. He forced her down on the cold tiled floor. She struggled as he ripped off her pantyhose, then tried to get away from him as he unbuckled his belt, pulled down his zipper, and dropped his pants to his knees. He was too strong and took her quickly. In seconds, it was over.

"Now you can go back to work," he said, getting up and smiling as he straightened his clothes.

"No, now I can go home and change clothes. What the hell did you think you were doing? That was the same thing as rape! I want you to know I didn't enjoy it one bit. It was dirty and ugly and you're a pig."

Jason slapped her face. "Don't hand me any shit. I'm not in the mood."

"The hell with you too, Jason. I'm going home to change clothes and take a shower. I really need a shower after that."

"Whatever you think you have to do. Just get back in here as soon as you're done, so we can finish tonight."

"I think we're already finished."

"Just get back here. We've got to get this proposal done."

She left the building, and Jason went back to work. Two hours went by before he realized she was gone too long. He called her at home. He didn't get an answer. How could she do this to him? Leaving him with all the work and needing it so bad again. He rubbed his hand across the front of his pants. That's the only thing women were good for. They sure didn't hold up their end as far as money was concerned. Where the hell was she? How was he going to be able to tolerate this from her? She was simply going to have to learn to do what he told her to do. Otherwise, she wasn't going to like the consequences.

Chapter 42

Jason was red-eyed and shaky from the many cups of coffee he drank during the long night, when Twilabee entered his office.

"Got the proposal done, Jason?"

"Everything except the final typing."

"Give it to Susan. I want it in an hour."

"She's not here."

"Where the hell is she?"

"Damned if I know. She took off not long after everyone else went home. I haven't seen her since."

"Her car's still in the lot. You must know where she went."

"She said she was going home to take a nap or whatever. She never came back. I've been in this office ever since. I could've used her help. I certainly don't appreciate her behavior."

"Nor do I. Call her at home and get her in here."

"I already have. Several times. She's not answering her phone. Not returning my calls."

"Get someone else on it. I want it on my desk as soon as possible."

"There's a lot here. How about putting two people on it?"

"I really don't care how you do it, Jason. I want this thing completed today."

Three hours later, the proposal was dropped on Twilabee's desk. He reviewed it, noted the changes he wanted, and shortly before noon, the final copy was in his hands. He called Gary Brown into his office.

"Call Ben Thomas and have him and his brother come in here," he told Gary, "so we can get this thing settled."

Gary went back to his office and called. Ben answered.

"We have a written proposal ready for you, Mr. Thomas," Gary explained, "and we would like to have you come in and look at it. Right away, if it's at all possible?"

"I ain't going no-damn-where. You want me to look at it, bring it out here. I honestly don't care if it ever gets done."

Ben hung up. Gary went back to Twilabee and told him what Ben's answer was.

"For Christ's sake," Twilabee roared, "can't anyone in this bank get anything done right! Give me his number. I'll call him."

Twilabee made the call and, this time, talked to Roy. He got the same answer, with several expletives added. It wasn't at all what he expected to hear and certainly wasn't what he was used to hearing. It made him realize he didn't have the upper hand this time. Thirty minutes later, they were on their way to the Thomas farm.

Ben politely invited them in when they got there, then offered them coffee. They accepted and sat down at the kitchen table. Twilabee let his eyes roam around the kitchen. His expression showed his surprise at what he saw.

Everything in the room was meticulously clean and in perfect order. A total contrast to the filthy mess he'd expected to find in a house with only men, dumb farmers at that, living in it.

Mack, who went for a walk in the refuge after doing the morning kitchen chores, joined them shortly after Twilabee began explaining what was in the proposal. Mack stood, leaning against the kitchen counter, without bothering to say hello. The proposal surprised him. It was a far better offer than Roy's most extravagant demands. He knew that historic preservation and demonstrating organic farming was little more than a publicity gimmick, coming from them. At the same time, he knew that with them leaving the actual farming operation up to Ben, there was a real chance of some good coming from their ideas. Getting Ben out of this barn of a house, which was costly to heat and in constant need of repair, was a big plus too. Especially since it was to be completely restored and preserved. It and the old barn.

"It sounds okay to me," Roy said when they finished. "Ben?"

"It's okay with me too, except one thing. My boy Mack here." Ben introduced Mack to the two men. "It's always been Mack's dream to take over this farm someday. This deal leaves him out in the cold. Can't say I like that much."

"I don't see that as a problem, Ben," Twilabee said. "You'll be in complete charge of the farming. We obviously need your expertise. So you have control over the personnel involved."

"What the hell are you talking about?"

"He means," Gary Brown said, "that you hire who you want to hire. You want Mack working with you, fine. You decide in what capacity. I could easily see him being assistant manager of the farming operation. You'll need one, and it might as well be him. In fact, it's to our advantage if it is him. He already knows the operation. It'll save us the training expense we'd have with someone who didn't."

"So long as the close family relationship isn't a problem," Twilabee added.

Roy laughed loudly, shaking his head.

"You dumb shit," he said, looking at Twilabee, "any damn fool can see what those two are. You ever get two people working together as good as they do, I want to meet them. Because it isn't very likely you ever will."

"Very well," said Twilabee, his face turning a deep red from being called a dumb shit and fool, "do we have an agreement?"

"What do you think, Mack?" Ben asked.

"It's fair. As long as you have a long-term contract for your job. For me, it'll depend on whether I can cut it or not. Go for it."

"Roy?"

"Go for it."

"Okay, Mr. Twilabee, we got a deal." Ben stuck out his hand, and the two men shook on it.

"Now that we've got a deal," Roy said, "you've got to understand we meant it when we told you to keep the contract simple. I know your lawyers have got to put it together and our lawyer's got to okay it, but if Ben, Mack, and I don't understand every word of it, the deal is off. We won't be screwing around reading more than one version. Understand?"

"We have to follow our lawyer's advice," Gary Brown complained.

"Bullshit! You got to want a deal or not. Ben's never cheated another man in his life. He'd die first. Keep the damn thing simple. Keep it honest. You do, and you'll find you cut yourself a hell of a deal. You don't, and you got no deal at all. Neither you nor Ben need some shit-talking lawyer screwing it up."

"We got the message," said Twilabee. "It will be straight and simple, or I'll fire the lawyers and get some new ones."

"The kind of talk I like to hear," Roy said.

"Is it okay if I say something?" Mack asked.

"About what?" Ben asked.

"The whole deal. Every bit of it."

"I got the feeling that if I say no, we'll all regret it. Go ahead, Mack, let them have it."

"It looks like," Mack said, his eyes focused on Twilabee's, "that I'm going to be part of this. I'll do it because I think you've come up with a few ideas that'll bring some good into your stinking resort. I still can't let you out of here without telling you I think the whole project should be scrapped, and the refuge should be preserved. What you're doing is basically wrong. It's immoral. No matter what happens, no matter what Dad or I ever gain, I'll never change my mind about your project. Any good it accomplishes will never come close to the wrong being done."

"After the money you people are making," Twilabee asked, "you can still say that?"

"I'm not part of this for money. Neither is Dad. We're taking your money to kick your ass some, not because we want it or need it. Dad will probably find a way to give it away somehow. I can't see him spending it on himself. He's got more than he wants or needs now. So have I, and I'm dead-ass broke."

Twilabee laughed. "I can't begin to understand you people or what the hell it is that motivates you," he said, "but I think I'm going to like working with you. I think I'm going to like it one hell of a lot. Have a good day now."

He walked out of the house with Gary Brown trailing behind him.

"Good speech," Ben said, grinning at Mack.

"Too short though," Roy said. "I was hoping you'd give them some real hellfire. You didn't even scream."

"I'm getting too old to waste a lot of talk where it doesn't do any good.

Chapter 43

Mack was anxious again while he waited for Mandy to get home. It started a full two hours before he expected her home and he wasn't able to control it, no matter how hard he tried. He couldn't think about anything else until Wanda made a surprise visit a short time before Mandy was due home.

"What's up?" he asked her.

"Nothing. Dale and I were going out, but he's working late tonight, so I thought I'd come by for a visit. It's so nice and quiet here compared to town. Besides, Mack, I knew Mandy wouldn't be home yet, so I'd get the chance to flirt, show you a little of what you passed up."

"Hell, Wanda, I know what I gave up. Never would have either, if Mandy and I hadn't been involved already. So why is Dale working? He's the boss now. He shouldn't have to work any overtime."

"I don't know. He usually tells me what's going on. Tonight, all he said was that it was serious. I think he might be looking for the girl from the bank."

"What girl? Why is Dale looking for her?"

"The one whose friend was killed in town last week. You've probably seen her, she's the receptionist at the bank part of the time. I think her name is Susan."

"I know who you mean," Mack answered, knowing she was the young woman Jason had an eye for the day he went to the bank to visit him. "What happened to her?"

"All I've heard is that she disappeared."

"When? How? Why?"

"What the hell are you so hyper about all the sudden, Mack? That's too many questions all at the same time, so give them to me one at a time."

"I'm sorry. When did this happen?"

"Last night. I heard she was working late. Her and Jason..."

"Jason was with Susan and Judy Geyser, the girl from the cities, who was murdered the other night."

"I know that, so stop interrupting me."

"Okay, Wanda, I'm sorry again."

"Anyway, she and Jason were working late on some big deal for the bank when she decided to go home for some reason. Nobody's seen her since. Except she left her car in the bank parking lot."

"Is that all you know?"

"That's about it, except Dale said Jason was a real smart-ass when he talked to him about Susan being gone."

"I hate this. Especially when it has to do with Jason. I've been going near crazy worrying about Mandy as it is." He looked at his watch. "It's about time for the news. Let's see if there's anything on about Susan's disappearance."

"Why the hell would they have it on? She isn't a kid, and we're way the hell away from the cities. Those television people don't care what happens here. Not unless it's some kind of horrible murder or something."

"At least it'll give me something to do besides worry."

"Take me to the woods out back," she giggled, "and I'll give you plenty to do."

"Now, Wanda, Dale wouldn't like it if we did that."

"Mandy either. Only I would, and you too, maybe, if you ever gave it a try."

"I'm sure I'd love it, if I didn't have commitments and promises. Let's watch the news. It'll give you something to do too, besides tempting me."

"Well, hallelujah, at least I tempt you."

"Yeah, Wanda, you do."

Mack turned on the television set early enough to catch the end of a talk show. The first commercial, after it ended, was for the news. All they said was "The body of woman was found today on a rural county road north of Minneapolis. Stay tuned to the news for details."

"Wow," Wanda said, "you don't think it was her, do you?"

It was. Mack was numb with worry after he knew, unable to do anything except sit and stare at a blaring box. He only had one thought. Would Mandy be next?

Ben and Roy came back from town a short time later, having heard the news as it spread through town. They tried to talk to Mack. He waved them off, telling them to leave him alone. They took Wanda into the kitchen with them and sweated it out there, hoping Mandy wouldn't be any later than expected. She wasn't, and within minutes of her getting there, Mack was his old self again. By the time Dale stopped by for Wanda, he was actually laughing at one of Roy's jokes.

"It's a bad deal," Dale said when they asked him about the girl. He told them it was Susan. "She was killed the same way as the other girl."

"What about Jason?" Mack asked, after Dale told them some of the details. "Do you think he did it?"

"There's no proof he did it, so there's nothing I can do to him yet. According to Gary Brown at the bank, he's sure Jason was there working all night. He had to be, to be able to get the proposal he was writing completed. You guys know how detailed it was for you. I don't have any way to know for sure what time she left the bank. The medical examiner said she died about nine or ten last night. He thought she was raped. She had a minor bruise on her cheek too, which wasn't part of the head injuries that killed her. Jason admitted having sex with her. There was no sign of anything violent happening at the bank, inside or out. So I don't know yet. Only that Jason was with both of the girls before they died."

"How's Jason acting?" Mack asked.

"Mostly, he's acting angry. Can't see how a fine Christian gentleman like himself can be taken to the police station and asked all those offensive questions. Claims last night was the first time he's ever had sex outside of marriage. The only reason it happened at all was because of the problems he's having with his wife, which you, Mack, caused."

"He's an absolute liar on both counts," Mack said.

"Yeah, I know, Jason's a total phony. We know without a doubt he's sleeping with the refuge lady. I wonder if she's next? According to some of the people at the bank, there's been rumors about Jason and Susan too."

"Knowing Jason," Mack said, "they're true."

"It isn't any of my business," Roy said, "but you two know he's capable of just about anything, no matter how evil. I'm real glad Mandy's living here now, and I think it's past the time Wanda moved out of her apartment. You got room for her, Dale? You haven't, she can come here." He smiled. "Hell, my bed will hold the both of us."

Dale turned red, unsure if Roy was joking or not. None of them were sure Roy was joking. Not even Ben.

"I..." Dale said, looking at Wanda, "I have room, if she wants to come."

Wanda dropped her eyes, then looked up at Mack. "I'll stay with you, Dale," she said, "so long as you understand it's only until this blows over. We have to wait a while before we talk about making anything permanent."

"I understand, Wanda. I only want you safe."

Dale left a short time later, complaining about having to go back to work yet knowing there was no choice. The rest of them spent the evening at the kitchen table, filling the time with quiet talk and watching Wanda and Roy flirt.

The rest of the week went by the same way. Mack a nervous wreck until Mandy was home, the evenings filled with quiet talk, short visits from Dale, and flirting.

Until Friday.

Chapter 44

Mandy buried herself in her work all day, barely taking time for coffee, hoping she'd catch up before she went home. It was five minutes before she was due there when she realized how late it was. She called Mack immediately.

"Don't worry," she told him, "I'm leaving right now. I'll be there in an hour. Maybe less if traffic isn't too bad."

"I'll worry anyway," he said. "So please be careful. I'll see you when you get home."

He knew he needed to do something to numb his mind, so he sat down with Wanda to watch television, knowing nothing would do the job as well as it could. Within minutes of turning the set on, there was a news flash about a five-car pileup on the northbound lanes of I494, Mandy's route home. She'd be later than she said she'd be, but he knew she couldn't be far enough north to be in the accident. He let himself get involved in a cop show rerun and stopped watching the clock. He was almost relaxed when he heard the siren. He leaped from the couch and ran to the back door, getting there as the flashing lights drove into the yard at a high speed.

It was Dale.

"We got to go, Mack," he yelled as Mack stepped outside. "It's Mandy."

Mack ran for the car, Wanda at his heels.

"I'm going along!" she said, diving into the back seat.

"Seat belts," Dale said, then was quiet until he reached the highway, using all his concentration to keep the car on the road. Once he was doing a steady one hundred miles an hour, he said, "Don't know the details. She was attacked. Found right away by a cop I know down there. I asked him to keep an eye on her and her car. Couldn't have been more than a couple of minutes after it happened that he found her. He called me as soon as he took care of her. She's on her way to, or she's at, Methodist Hospital. That's where we're going, and that's all I know."

The rest of the ride was nightmare filled with the screaming siren and flashing lights. Mack felt like he was again living the terror he hadn't yet managed to rid his nights of. Julie. Julie was in an accident, and now she was dead. What would he do if he lost Mandy? Was it going to be the same way with her as it was with Julie? Would Mandy die? How could this be happening again? No. No! Please, let her live! If she didn't, how could he?

She had to live!

Dale dropped him at the emergency entrance. He ran inside and was directed to the desk. They told him she was in surgery, and he'd have to wait. He waited, pacing back and forth, trying to walk the nightmare away. Dale called Ben and Roy as soon as he and Wanda were inside. Wanda finally talked Mack into sitting down next to her. She held his hand, trying to calm him, wishing she could comfort him. Dale sat down on the other side of Wanda, studying the ceiling and then the floor. When they finally let Mack see Mandy, the doctor told him it didn't look good.

"What does that mean?" Mack asked.

"Her neck is broken, and she has several other injuries."

Wanda started crying. Dale put his arms around her in a feeble effort to comfort her and ease her pain.

"How bad is it?" Mack asked, unable to comprehend what he heard. "Real bad. She's conscious now." The doctor touched Mack's shoulder, pointing him in Mandy's direction. "I suggest you go in and see her while you still can."

When he entered the curtained-off area where they'd put her, Mandy was trying to smile through her bandaged face. There were tubes plugged into her everywhere. Mack took her hand, squeezed it, and felt a slight pressure from hers.

"I love you," he said.

"Love you too," she answered, gasping for breath with every word. "I don't think it was Jason. It was someone smaller. Stronger." Her voice was barely a whisper. "Please, Mack," she pleaded, "Don't let hate rule you now. I want you to have a life. I always loved you."

Gasping for air, she struggled for a deep breath but didn't release it. She died.

Mack collapsed, dropping to the floor.

Chapter 45

Ben hung up the phone so carefully it seemed as though he was afraid of breaking it. He turned to Roy.

"They're leaving the hospital now. Mack's not taking it well. The doctor's sending some sleeping pills along with Wanda for him. Might be the only way to get him through this. Wish I still had some crops. Lots of work would be a good thing right now."

"The kid's sure had more than his share of hard knocks. I'd guess we better be ready for a long haul, getting him through this one. It appeared to me that he and Mandy were made for each other. Awful hard thing for him to lose her. I'm not sure I could handle it if I were him."

"It had to happen now, when Mack was finally finding himself. So was Mandy in her own way. For the first time, they had what they needed to make a life. It was a long time coming for those two."

"Yeah, they must have been carrying what they felt inside all those years. Going to be hard, keeping him from killing Jason."

"Don't know that I'd mind killing Jason myself, if he was worth killing. Not for me, for damn sure not for Mack, and not for you either, Roy. Mack's going to be needing you as bad as me. There hasn't ever been anyone he's looked up to more than you. So you aren't going to help him if you get yourself locked up for something so stupid as killing the likes of Jason."

"Stop your worrying on it, Ben. If I was thinking he was worth killing, I'd be out hunting now. The law can handle him. So long as they do it right."

"Good. Now let's figure out how we're going to get our boy through this."

The two men sat at the kitchen table, sipping coffee, talking, making frequent glances at the clock on the wall, trying to wait out the forever hour it took their boy to come home. When they got there, Wanda held Mack's arm as they moved slowly from the car to the house. His head sagged. When he got close, they could see his red sunken eyes. He moved as though most of the life had been taken out of him.

Wanda led him to the living room couch, and he dropped onto it, kicking his legs straight out, staring up at the ceiling. Dale came in long enough to apologize for having to go back to work, then left.

Ben watched Mack for a few moments before asking, "Anything I can get you, son?"

Mack shook his head no.

"I know there's not a damn thing I can say to give you any comfort right now. You want me to leave you be for a while?"

Mack nodded his head.

Ben went back to the kitchen. Mack sat there, staring at the ceiling, trying to blot the horror out of his head, until he felt as though he couldn't breathe. He suddenly stood, knowing he had to get out and breathe fresh, clean, outside air. He needed to walk...had to walk out where there was real life around him. Where there was a purpose to life and death. Where, for a brief moment, he could get away from the stench of human life.

"Please," he said, going into the kitchen, "I need to go outside and walk. Let me go alone. I won't do anything stupid. I need to walk, I need to think, I need to breathe. I can't in here. I won't be gone long."

"Don't know that it's a good idea," Ben said, "you being alone, wandering around out there in the dark."

"I don't think so, either," Wanda agreed.

Roy paused a moment, studying Mack's face. Finally, he said, "I think it's okay. He gets out in those woods, he might find some sense to life he'll never find in here. The moon's bright tonight, so there's enough light to see by. Go ahead, Mack. Just be careful you're not gone too long. You'll worry these two to their end if you are."

"Thanks, Roy," Mack said and went outside.

He stopped in the yard, staring up at the moon and stars, wondering if part of Mandy was up there somewhere. He didn't have any of the comfort of religious beliefs yet hoped that somehow her beauty and spirit were still around. He shook his head, trying to stop the tears blinding his eyes, and started walking, with no special direction or destination. Only toward the refuge. His refuge.

He crossed the river, not knowing or caring how deep it was. He pushed his way through thickets, heavy with thorns ripping at his hands and arms, barely feeling the deep scratches they left. He turned north on a maintenance road when he came to it, blindly letting it lead him along. The pain of the many scratches he was beginning to feel couldn't bring him out of the far deeper pain inside. His sense of loss was so strong that nothing, he was sure, ever could.

Until he heard the voices. Familiar voices. A man and a woman. Jason and a woman. Jason, who killed Mandy or had Mandy killed, was out here with another woman, probably screwing his brains out. Polluting Mack's refuge by doing it.

A rage seized Mack, ripping deep into him, blotting out his pain, masking everything except the voices. Steadily, quietly, he crept closer to them, stopping when he was next to the van. There was no car, only the refuge van.

The woman was Elaine. Rich's face flashed through Mack's brain, building on his rage. What they were doing was an affront to his decency too. Mack was ready to kill them but forced himself to hold back so he could listen to their happy chatter.

"One way or the other," Elaine said, "I'm done with Rich tomorrow. We don't need him now. We've used him all we can. The impact study is written and ready to mail. No matter what I have to do to be free of him, tomorrow is the end of it."

"What's your hurry, Elaine? I'm still married."

"No, you aren't. Not any longer."

"Don't be silly. Now roll over, let's see what I can do with this."

"Okay, do it. I'm not silly. I'm ready."

It was all Mack could listen to. He opened the back doors of the van, grabbed the naked Jason by the ankles, and dragged him face down out of the van.

Jason screamed as his erect penis scraped the rough edges of the van's bumper, ripping open the skin. He wilted instantly and was bleeding profusely as Mack stepped back to let him get up.

"I'm going to bleed to death!" Jason screamed.

"She's dead, Jason," Mack said, ignoring his cries. "The same as you're going to be. Only difference is, I'm going to give you a chance."

"What the hell are you talking about?" Jason asked, holding himself as he struggled to his feet. "Jesus Christ, Mack, I'm going to bleed to death. I can't fight."

"Mandy's dead. Now you're going to die. You can fight or not. I'm killing you either way."

Elaine leaped from the rear of the van, nude, with a tire iron in her hand, swinging it over her head, a look of madness on her face. "I killed her, you dumb son of a bitch! I killed all three of those sluts who were tempting my Jason. And Ray too, like Jason wanted. I'm killing you now! I missed you before in the alley. I won't this time. Jason's mine, and I can't let you hurt him or let anyone screw him again either!"

She continued to swing the tire iron back and forth with both hands, aiming at Mack's head. When she was close enough to hit him, he ducked at the last second, feeling the air move inches above his head. He came up fast with a wild right hand, catching the side of her head. She started to go down, and Mack lashed out with his foot, his boot hitting her bare chest. She fell backward hard, her head making a solid thump against a rock. She lay there, as still as the rock.

"For god's sake, Mack!" Jason screamed. "You killed her!"

"Do you really think I care?" Mack asked, moving in on Jason. "You're next. It's past time you paid."

The fear in Jason's eyes told Mack he'd fight. Mack realized, as he moved in an ever tighter circle around Jason, that he had to be careful with his back, so it didn't go into spasms. He couldn't make any fancy moves. Simply stand up straight until Jason left an opening.

Mack continued to move in until in desperation, Jason charged him with his fists moving like pistons. Mack moved his hands in front of his face, his arms tight over his chest, letting Jason hit him and wear himself out. Mack knew he should feel pain from the rapid blows, but his anger and hatred dulled it.

He focused completely on Jason, whose flabby banker's arms quickly tired. It only took one opening, and Mack's strong left hand, so used to hanging on to an angry bull, hit Jason square on the nose, staggering him as blood sprayed over his face. Before Jason could gain his balance, Mack's right hand came flying upward, catching him under the chin. Jason was unconscious before his bare ass touched the ground.

Mack picked up a small boulder, raised it over his head, and set himself to bring it down hard on Jason's head. He hesitated, staring down at the bleeding piece of garbage, rapidly losing the desire to kill it.

Suddenly, a sharp pain ripped deep into his shoulder. He dropped the rock and turned toward its source. Elaine was raising the tire iron in her hands, ready to hit him again. He leaped away, and she only grazed his arm. Before she could hit him again, he jumped her, wrestling her to the ground and trying to hold her down, horrified now that he was fighting with a naked woman.

Her strength was incredible, and she threw him off. He rolled away and was on his feet before she managed to stand. He lashed out with his foot and was lucky enough to kick the tire iron out of her hand. Enraged, she was all over him, her clawed fingers raking across his face, then her fists swinging so wildly that she constantly missed her target. He lost his qualms about the fight as he stepped back out of her reach, knowing now he had no choice.

Stretching his long left arm, he rapidly chopped at her face with it. Although his arm was weakened by the blow to his shoulder, he held her off long enough to connect with his right. She started to go down, then regained her balance and charged him again, landing a solid right in his stomach, nearly taking the wind out of him. He backed away, jabbing her in the face several times with his constantly weaker left, wondering where her strength was coming from, knowing he had to finish her soon or she'd find a way to kill him. Then she tried to duck under his left to get to his stomach again and stepped into a hard right, splitting her upper lip open. She touched the blood streaming out of her mouth, screamed, and charged him again. He feinted a move to his right, jumped quickly left, and caught her in the stomach with a roundhouse right. She grunted loudly, and her hands dropped to her side yet somehow managed to stay upright. He quickly moved in, pounding her stomach with both hands until she finally doubled over. When she did, he grabbed her black hair, and with all the strength he had left in him, he pulled her head down and brought his knee up into her face. He let her go, and she remained where she was for a moment, then toppled over, still conscious, but unable to move.

Now, as suddenly as it rushed over him, his anger disappeared. He no longer cared about Jason, who was merely a pathetic pile of nothing, lying there bleeding, and he cared even less about his insane whore, Elaine. They meant nothing at all to him. All he felt was complete contempt. He couldn't bring Mandy back by killing them. He couldn't bring her back no matter what he did. He knew he had to live with it. Now he knew he could. It would be hard, it would take time, but he could and he would.

He looked over at Elaine, who was stirring back to life. Even though she was the one who killed Mandy, the poor stupid girl from the bank, and the innocent girl from the cities, the desire to hurt her more than he already had was gone.

Mack almost smiled as he turned toward home, no longer blinded by pain or rage. His heart was still heavy, Mandy was still gone and his refuge soon would be, but he could live now. He'd find his place, somehow, somewhere. No matter what people like the monsters he was leaving behind him did. No matter what happened to them now.

Chapter 46

Elaine sat up slowly, her head pounding, still dazed from Mack's blows. She looked over at Jason, then searched the ground with her eyes for the tire iron, hoping to use it on Mack as soon as she could stand. She concentrated on it so hard she didn't see Rich step out of the brush in front of her. He had followed her again, then lost her on the curving road. This was the third open gate he'd checked. At the other two, he'd sent the teenagers he found home. He'd only been there long enough to watch Mack walk away.

"Hello, dear," Rich said softly, so Mack wouldn't hear him. "Have a good time tonight?"

"Why are you here?" she asked, without caring what his answer would be.

"I followed you here, dear."

He grabbed her by the hair, pulling her head back so he could see her mangled face and look into her evil eyes.

"Tell me why." Rich said, shaking her head with his hand. "Why did you do it? Why did you kill Ray?"

"It was my job, and Jason wanted me to do it," she answered, her voice a weak monotone, without a trace of emotion. "They sent me out here to get you and Ray to write the impact study the way they needed it to be written, so they could get the deal done for the project." She paused to take a deep breath, then continued in the same flat tone. "You were so easy. All I had to do was my magic and marry you. Ray wouldn't agree. Not even for my magic, no matter how much he liked it. He was easy to kill anyway. He caught me going through his files. So I did my magic to him, and like he always did at the right time, he opened his mouth. He never knew it was coming until the sheriff pushed the gun in his mouth. My magic got the job done, the way Jason said it would. Jason always knows how to get things done."

Rich was almost sick, listening to her. He shook her head again, harder this time.

"What about the girls? Did you kill them?"

"I did it for Jason. They were tempting him, making him do bad things. I couldn't let them do that. He's mine. They were whores. So I killed them."

"Did you know, do you know, that the first girl never had a thing to do with Jason, other than having a couple of drinks? Jason slept with the girl Susan the night you killed the first girl. The cops proved it already."

"I don't care. She should have stayed farther from Jason than she did. I'll kill her again, if she comes near him again. I'll kill everyone as many times as I have to. Jason's mine. I liked killing them. It felt so good when I hit them."

Rich stared at the insanity in her glazed-over eyes, then gave her head one more shake. He dropped her hair and turned away from her, hoping he could walk away from her the way Mack did. He couldn't, and he turned toward her again. Her eyes opened wide with shock when she saw his big boot fly up at her head. She didn't have the time or strength left to duck. His foot slammed into her, landing under her chin, snapping her head back violently, breaking her neck. Only her eyes followed him when he moved.

Rich looked at Jason, thinking about using the rock Mack had picked up to smash his head in. He decided not to bother. He opened the back of the van and took out the spade that was always carried in refuge vans and trucks.

"You two," Rich said to himself, "had to have your lake here where there shouldn't be one. Now you can spend forever with it."

He walked to the sandy edge of the river and started digging, going down about four feet. Jason groaned as Rich dragged him to the hole and dumped him in. He still wasn't conscious enough to struggle. He groaned again when Rich pushed Elaine in on top of him. She stared up at him until he dropped their clothes over them, covering her face. Jason didn't stop moaning until Rich had the hole half full of the cold river sand. Elaine never made a sound.

When the hole was filled, Rich moved enough rocks over the top of it and on the ground near it to keep the river from washing it open, even in a heavy rainstorm. He broke a branch off some brush and used it to erase all the footprints he could find, concentrating on eliminating the tracks Mack had made. It was easy because fifty feet down the maintenance road, the ground was so hard Mack hadn't left any tracks.

Rich threw the broken branch far out in the river and stood watching it float downstream until it was out of sight. He drove the van back to the refuge maintenance area and parked it in its proper spot.

He laughed when a storm suddenly hit, with heavy rain and strong wind gusts, during his walk back to the river to get his truck. Nobody would ever know what really happened. All sign of anyone being there, where Jason and Elaine were going to spend an eternity, was gone. Now he was free. Free to do what he should have done from the start.

He could fight them now. The hell with the job. The real environmental impact study, the one he and Ray wrote, was going to be filed. And not only in Washington. It was going to every major newspaper and television station he could think of. With a long letter explaining it. Maybe he couldn't stop their resort, but he sure could raise a lot of hell, and maybe he could stop them from destroying the rest of this refuge. Let them have the south leg.

They weren't going to destroy the whole thing. The one thing in his life he worked so hard for, for so many years, that he loved so much.

Chapter 47

Everyone was upset when Mack got back to the farm. Wanda was horrified over his many scratches and bruises, but they were relieved to have him home.

Mack told them what happened as Wanda nursed his wounds. As he did, Roy saw life coming back into his eyes. By the time he finished, Roy knew Mack would be okay, that the pain inside him was already beginning to heal. To be sure Ben and Wanda saw the same thing, Roy laughed, then looked Mack in the eye,

"You make this old uncle of yours proud, boy," he said, "real proud. There's no way you could've done it better."

"Even beating the hell out of a woman?"

"She isn't a woman, she's a psychopathic killer. You sure can't call what you did abuse or any such thing. Not when you're fighting for your life. As far as I'm concerned, she was lucky that's all you did. I believe I'd of killed her, female or not."

"I'm glad you didn't kill them, Mack," Wanda said. "It's better this way."

"Sure it is," Roy agreed. "Nothing you did was wrong."

"That's for sure the truth," Ben agreed.

Mack gave them a small grin and nodded.

Knowing then that Mack was going to be okay, that he'd make it through this, Ben took the time to call Dale. He came over right away.

After Mack filled Dale in on all the details, he went out in the rain to make a thorough search of the area where Mack said he fought with Jason and Elaine. Dale didn't find a trace of them or anything else. Dale returned to the farm, unsure whether or not he'd found the right spot, so he and several deputies searched again in the morning. They still couldn't find any sign of anyone being there or that anything had happened. Even Dale's tracks were washed away then, by the all-night rain.

The van was found parked outside in the refuge maintenance area. The rain washed it so clean they couldn't find any trace of Jason's blood, which Mack was sure was on the rear bumper. Jason's car was found in the bank's parking area. Elaine's at her home. No other sign of them was found.

"It's all a little too perfect," Dale said when he talked to all of them on Sunday afternoon, the day after the search. "How could they disappear so completely? They didn't fly out or take a bus. No personal items appear to be missing from either of their homes. They're not in any hospital around here or in the cities. From what you told me, Mack, that's where they both ought to be."

"Maybe they're dead," Wanda said, grinning. "Maybe someone else came along and killed them and buried them by the river." She laughed.

"Sure, Wanda. Someone walks through the woods, finds them beaten up, kills them, and buries them. Don't be ridiculous."

"Well hell, it would be the best way for it to end."

"Just too unlikely to ever consider."

"What does Rich think happened?" Mack asked.

"He didn't have any idea. We had to wake him up to talk to him. Seems he drank too much the night before. Didn't even know Elaine was gone until we got there. It took him a while to react because he had one hell of a hangover. He was pretty broken up when he found out what Elaine was involved in. That she actually committed those murders. I don't think he's going to be able to help us at all. No one at the bank has any ideas, either."

"Well," Mack said, "if you talk to them again, would you do me a favor?"

"Sure, just name it."

"Ask Gary Brown why they decided to build their resort here. It seems to me that they could've found other places for it."

"I already asked him, Mack. You've made me think a lot about the project and the refuge. I'm beginning to believe you were right all along. Money will never buy what we're throwing away out there."

"So what did Gary tell you were the reasons for building it here?"

"Simple economics. Money. The refuge is close to the cities. Closer than any other spot with everything this area has to offer. A big resort, with all the amenities and so close to the cities, will be a gold mine. People will be able to take a real vacation without any heavy transportation costs or time wasted traveling. Just take a short drive to heaven. Early on, they'll have more customers than facilities. So they don't plan on stopping with the south leg of the refuge. They're hoping to have it all eventually, taking it a piece at a time. Unless they're stopped, which this time, I think they will be."

"I hope so. Where do you go from here?"

"I'll keep looking for Jason and Elaine. They're wanted for murder now. I don't honestly think we'll ever find them. I'm just glad it wasn't you who made them disappear. We'll keep digging too, learning as much as we can about what happened. Finding proof, besides the blood on the tire iron we found in the back of Elaine's van. There was blood left, by the way, from all three of her victims. We have definite matches on all of them. We still want to find as much additional evidence as possible, to prove she and Jason are the guilty ones."

"I guess that's all you can do."

"It all too often is."

Mack thought about their mysterious disappearance after Dale left, then quickly put it out of his mind. He no longer cared what happened to them, even though he was sure they panicked and ran. If they were ever caught, it would be fine with him. It was no longer a personal thing. Either way, Mandy was still gone. He knew, deep inside, that no matter what anyone said or did, the refuge soon would be.

Humans, he knew without a doubt, would continue to destroy their planet until they destroyed themselves. Greed and ignorance would see to it. It was too bad they'd never understand that the refuge and all places like it weren't only for the trees and animals and all the wild things. They were refuges for the human spirit. The real spirit that respected and made sense out of life. Not the artificial ideas and beliefs the religious, business, and political communities were always so eager to preach. There was no spirit in them. Their only purpose was to satisfy the need to control and rape, not only the environment, but the human spirit as well.

Epilogue

Mandy was cremated, as had been her wish. There was a memorial service for her several days later.

Mack went to it, although he'd have preferred not to. It was a hot, humid day, yet Mack felt chilled from the cold sweat seeping from every pore when he entered the church. He sat near the front, with Ben, Roy, Wanda, and Dale.

Wanda started crying, even before the service started, and Ben, Roy, and Dale had tears in their eyes shortly after it began. Mack sat ramrod straight, his face made of stone, even though his heart was breaking.

The church was crowded, filled with family and friends, and some of Jason's relatives, the few who felt they could afford to miss a day of work. Mack did his best to ignore them, and with the exception of one of Jason's cousins, he did. He acknowledged her with a brief nod when she smiled and waved at him. He couldn't force himself to return her smile. He liked Beth when they were kids, and he and Mandy had doubled with her and Jason a couple of times. Even so, Mack knew he couldn't bring himself to talk to her.

The beginning of the service was bearable, even though the music was typically Lutheran, drab noise, and those few who spoke about Mandy stuttered and stammered, while saying little.

When the minister got up in the pulpit, it was obvious he didn't know Mandy when he talked about her. It became unbearable to Mack when he used the service as an opportunity to preach. The last thing Mack needed to hear was the nonsense about the glories of dying and going to heaven. If dying was really that great, why didn't the preacher go outside and shoot himself? It would, Mack was sure, improve the planet if he did.

Mack somehow made it through the service, feeling a great sense of relief when it was time to go. Before he managed to get out of the church, he was surprised by Mandy's mother. She approached him, carrying a brass urn.

"These, Mack," she said, struggling to control her tears, "are Mandy's ashes. I want you to have them, to do with them what you think is best."

"What…why? Why me?"

"Because she loved you so much. She called me nearly every day after you two found each other again. I don't think she was ever as happy as she was those last days. She certainly wasn't happy before you came home. You gave her so much joy. She loved you deeply, Mack. Few of us ever know a love so strong or so real."

"I don't know…"

"I know, Mack, that you don't know now what to do with them. You will, in time, after you think about it. Somewhere, there's a place where the two of you were the happiest. I want her to rest there."

She reached up, touched his cheek, then turned and walked away. Mack marveled at her control.

* * *

It was early morning, well before sunrise, when Rich got to the refuge headquarters. It was quiet, with no wind, not even the rustle of tree leaves broke the silence around him. He felt his chest swell as he sucked in as much of the clean air as possible. As he exhaled, he wondered how he could have ever let anything or anyone convince him it would be okay to destroy any part of this place, which always refreshed his spirit and restored his soul.

He left most of the lights off when he went inside and made his way into the office where the computer was. There he called up all the files holding the latest environmental impact study. Rich erased them all. Next, he took out all the backup disks and destroyed them. The paper copies, packaged and ready to mail, he took out in the parking lot. The small fire they made, after he poured gasoline over them, did wake a few birds and start them singing.

After the fire burned itself out, he cleaned up the ashes, leaving no sign of it. Going back inside, he printed new copies of the impact study he and Ray Foss had originally written, using disk copies he'd carefully hidden when he was told to destroy them. He packaged his impact printout copies the same way as those he burned had been and put them in the outgoing mail bin. No one would know, with the packages in the bin, that his study was going out until it was too late.

He went home and left a message on the headquarters voice mail saying he was sick and wouldn't be in that day. He went back to bed and slept peacefully, without dreams or guilt, with the knowledge he'd be mailing a lot more copies of his study. None of those, however, would be going to Washington.

* * *

Mack walked out into the refuge a few days later, watching the sunrise as he did. He stopped in the small stand of pines, on the ridge overlooking the river where he and Mandy spent one of their last times together. It was the right spot to let her go. It would soon be destroyed, but the memory of it, just as the memory of her, would never leave him.

He sat down, his back resting against a huge pine tree, waiting, and watching the life around him unfold in the bright sunlight. He stayed there, unmoving, until midmorning when a breeze came up. He stood, walked to the edge of the ridge, and spread her ashes in the wind. A light gust caught them, carrying them over a wide expanse of the refuge.

"Goodbye, Mandy," he said, watching the ashes ride on the wind. "If you can hear me, wherever you are now, please know that I always loved you too."

With that, he turned and walked away. It would be the last time he'd ever see that place as it was.

* * *

As Mack asked her to do, Wanda began packing Mandy's things. She tried to pay attention to what she was doing, but her thoughts were on Mack. She worried about him constantly, while at the same time, she was sure he'd be okay. With a family as strong as his, it'd be difficult for him not to be. Just being a friend of this family made her stronger. Even so, she longed to be a permanent part of it.

Because her thoughts nearly blotted out what she was doing, she almost ignored the large envelope on the bottom of one of the dresser drawers she was emptying. It said Harley Anderson on the front. Wanda gave it a quick look. Even though it was sealed, she could tell that there were computer disks and some papers inside. She thought about showing it to Mack, then decided instead to give it to Dale when he stopped by that afternoon. He could drop it off at Harley's home when he was out patrolling.

* * *

Mack knew when he left the refuge that he'd have to leave now and find a new place to live. Home was too close to Mandy. He needed to be in a place far away or he wouldn't find the strength to let her go. Until he did, he knew he couldn't rebuild the broken pieces of his life.

He started packing as soon as he got home. Roy didn't say a word when he saw what Mack was doing. He simply walked away.

"You can't go this way," Ben argued as he watched Mack fill a small suitcase. "Let me buy you a truck and give you some cash. There isn't any sense in you needing to fight just to get a meal. I've got more money now than I'll ever need. Take some of it with you."

"I know you mean well, Dad. I just think it will be better if I do without for a while. It will keep my mind on the right things. If I don't have the time to dwell on the wrong things, maybe I won't."

"This isn't right, Mack."

"Don't worry, if I get into any situation where I need you, I will yell for help."

Shortly before Mack was ready to leave, Dale stopped by to see Wanda, so he and Mack had the chance to say a quick goodbye, then Dale spent the rest of his short time there with Wanda.

She argued with Mack too, when he was ready to go. But his mind was made up. He was going alone, with nothing other than the hundred-dollar bill Ben stuffed into his shirt pocket. This time, though, after he gave Wanda a goodbye hug, he remembered to give his father one. His uncle too. The three of them stood watching from the farmyard as he walked away, carrying his one small suitcase.

"Damn it to hell, Roy," Ben said, "how can we let him go like this? I watched you leave like this once. That hurt. This is killing me."

"I made out okay, didn't I, Ben?" Roy paused a moment. "We ain't going to let him do it anyway." He pulled a key out of his pocket and handed it to Wanda. "This is for the house on my ranch. There's a map on how to get there tucked behind the visor of your car. Give her some money, Ben, she'll be needing clothes and such. The people down there, who watch the place for me, will know you're coming. I know you love him, so go take care of our boy. He needs you a lot more than he knows."

"Call Dale and tell him," she said. "And thank you both. You're the greatest dads I've ever seen."

She hugged them, then gave Roy a kiss he wouldn't soon forget. She gave them a little wave goodbye just before she tore out of the driveway as fast as she dared, hoping Mack didn't get too far.

Dale wasn't surprised by the call. Most of Wanda's clothes were still there, even though she hadn't been there since the night Mandy died. He'd known from the start and had the knowledge reaffirmed that afternoon, that her feelings for Mack were stronger than anything she felt for him. Early on, he'd hoped she'd change her mind. Now that there was almost no chance she ever would, he didn't know whether he should feel relieved or cry.

Either way, he knew he'd always care for Wanda, and he hoped, above all else, that the horror would soon be over for his good friend Mack.

Mack didn't get far before Wanda found him. Only to the first tar road. He was wondering which direction to go when he reached the four-lane highway up ahead when she pulled alongside him and stopped. He stood there shaking his head, wishing he wouldn't have to reject her again. He'd already given her enough grief and pain. She slid over to the passenger side and opened the door.

"Get in," she said.

"You know I can't."

"Hell no, I don't know that. Get in and we'll talk some, then if you still want to do this alone, I'll drop you off and go home. Now get in."

"What about Dale?"

"He's known all along how I feel."

Mack reluctantly got in the car. "I know you don't understand why I have to do this," he said. "I just can't see any other way."

"I know you can't, Mack, even if you should. I know you've got a lot of healing to do. It's going to be twice as hard trying to do it alone. I've got the key to Roy's ranch house. He's calling the people down there who watch it for him when he's gone to tell them we're coming. He says there's enough work to keep you busy for as long as you want. He said a lot of real hard work will do you more good than anything else. It'll help you heal quicker than going hungry will."

"Did he tell you what he wants done?"

"He said you'd figure it out. Now listen to me, Mack. Let me take you there. If you ever want me to leave, I'll go. You need someone. Damn it, you need me! I can't replace Mandy and I won't ever try. I'll just be there for you, and I can hold you on those awful nights when the dreams come."

"What about you? You could have a good life with Dale. He's a real good man. He really cares about you. What do you want with a broken-down cowboy who'll probably never have much of a future? Hell, right now, I can barely feed us."

"Fuck it," she said, smiling. "We'll eat when we get to Texas."

They did.

Lightning Source UK Ltd.
Milton Keynes UK
UKHW040934250620
365293UK00034B/126/J